I0704093

OLD BONES

VOL. 2., 2024

The Henlo Press

Copyright © 2025 by The Henlo Press
All rights reserved.

This is a work of fiction. Names, characters, businesses, places, events, locales, and incidents are either the products of the author's imagination or used in a fictitious manner. Any resemblance to actual persons, living or dead, or actual events is purely coincidental.

This book or any portion thereof may not be reproduced or used in any manner whatsoever without the express written permission of the publisher, except for the use of brief quotations in a book review.

Printed in the United States of America
First Printing, 2025
Paperback ISBN: 978-1-962019-21-7

THE CLOSERS

AMANDA HOOSER

"Okay, okay. Well, if we're going back in time, then I've got a story for you," Mel said as she pulled her lawn chair closer to the fire pit. "But first, let me ask, have any of you ever heard of the Burger Chef murders?"

A review of the faces gathered around the campfire showed a negative consensus and Mel continued with her story. "Well, don't feel bad, I hadn't either until I started working at Patty's Pizza Shack in high school. Now, these murders took place back in the late seventies but my older brother, you guys remember Jason, right? Anyway, he'd studied the case in one of his criminal justice classes and couldn't wait to tell me all about it when I got the job. The short version is that four kids, two girls and two boys, were closing at a Burger Chef one Friday night, and one of their friends, who also worked there, stopped in to like, chit-chat with them, you know. The doors were unlocked but no one was there. This dude calls the cops because he knows that's not right, and when the cops get there they see that the safe is open and the place is empty. So, the cops think the kids have just taken the money to go party and they're like, well, kids will be kids. And that's as much effort as they put into investigating it."

"Wait, wait, I think I remember this one," Ryan said from across the firepit. "I didn't remember the name of the restaurant, but weren't the girls' purses still there?"

"Yes! So you know that no chick in her right mind, party or not, is leaving her purse behind," Mel confirmed. "So, anyway, the morning shift comes in, cleans the store, and everyone returns to business as usual. Except all four kids have disappeared. They don't come back home, they don't show up at work, they're just gone. And then they find one of the kids' cars, abandoned on the side of the road."

"And then they found the bodies," Ryan contributed.

"Exactly. Kidnapped, shot, and left in the woods. And by the time they realized the kids hadn't just run away of their own volition, the crime scene had been scrubbed clean several times and the whole thing was a huge mess. So, when I started this new job at the age of sixteen, my brother couldn't wait to tell me this whole freaking horror story that had happened almost twenty years before."

"Just to scare you," Angie said to Mel's right, leaning forward and poking at the fire with a stick.

"Yeah, because that's what big brothers do, or something. Anyway, because I was still in high school I couldn't work mornings, obviously, I always closed up at night. I thought about being kidnapped and murdered every single shift. Thank you, Jason.

"Anyway, so now that you are clued in as to my frame of mind, let me tell you about this one night of spectacular stupidity. It was me, April, Ronnie, and Chris closing up."

"Chris? Wait, Chris Jenkins? Wasn't that the guy you were madly in love with senior year?" Stacy asked while digging out another marshmallow to roast.

"Oh yeah. Madly, deeply in love. Honestly, I think half the class had a crush on him."

"Oh, you can firmly put me in that column," Angie agreed, laughing as she settled back into her lawn chair.

"Hell, me too," Ryan laughed, holding up his beer in salute.

"Well, you, my friend," Mel tilted her beer in Ryan's direction, "would have had better luck. He ended up dating Ronnie after we graduated."

"Damn it, I missed my chance," Ryan lamented before getting a good-natured smack on the arm from his husband, Danny.

"Anyway, so the whole point of this story..."

"Finally," Stacy said, tossing a marshmallow at her.

"Anyway... so Jason has instilled this fear in me that we're all going to be murdered, right? So, I remember it was October because we were making the jack-o-lantern pizzas, it's closing time and we've finally gotten rid of all of the customers. Ronnie was vacuuming the dining room, Chris was cleaning restrooms, April was mopping the kitchen, and I'd finished putting the food away and was taking the trash out.

"The dumpster was out back and had this half-ass fence made out of cheap wooden lattice surrounding it to make it look more attractive or something. It was a giant pain because it had a padlock and you had to unlock it and then move the door," Mel said, using her fingers to make air quotes at the word 'door.' "It was hard to open because the ground wasn't level and it always got stuck on this bump in the blacktop... anyway, a total pain.

"Now, the dumpster was up against a hillside and behind it was nothing but a few acres of woods and fuck all else. In the back of my mind, I always had this fear that some random hobo would come down out of the forest and be hiding behind the dumpster. I hated the nights that I was on garbage duty."

"Why didn't you just have the guys do it?" Angie asked.

"Right, like I was going to admit that I was scared? Remember, I had a crush! I was trying to impress Chris with how tough I was."

"Oh, honey," Rob snorted.

"You can shut it, buddy. Anyway, here I am, shoving this rolling bin across the blacktop in the cold, and those little plastic wheels are really loud on asphalt, so I didn't notice anything until I was right up to the enclosure. When I stopped and started to go around the bin to unlock the padlock, that's when I heard it." Pausing for effect, Mel took a swig of her own beer.

"I could hear rustling in the leaves. Remember, it was fall so there's like, dead leaves everywhere, and it sounded like someone was walking around in there. Now, already being programmed to assume that one day someone was going to jump out of the woods and try to kill me, let me tell you, I did not stick around to find out who it was.

"I took off *sprinting* for the back door, and of course, because it was windy, the mop that I'd propped it open with had fallen over. The door had shut and automatically locked. So, now, there was a psycho killer waiting on me in the garbage bin and I'd locked myself out of the building. I beat on the door for a second, and when no one answered, I took off running for the front door. But, I'm in a hurry, right? So, instead of running out onto the parking lot where I'd be visible to murderers, I decided to take off through the landscaping. The shrubbery would be better cover, right? I made it about five steps before I tripped over a sprinkler head and landed face first in the mulch."

Stacy leaned forward, laughing as she held out her stick towards Mel. A freshly roasted marshmallow was speared on the tip. "Here, you need this more than I do."

Mel accepted the marshmallow as tribute. "I do, thank you. Anyway, I picked my ass up out of the mulch and continued to scurry to the front of the building where all of the big windows were. Now, as you are probably aware, if you are indoors, the lights are on, and it's dark outside, the only thing you can see is your own damn self. So, here I am, pounding on the window by the front door, and not only can no one see me, but Ronnie is still running the freaking vacuum on the other side of the room and can't hear me. So, I run around the entire front of the building and start banging and waving my arms on the side he's facing until I finally get his attention."

"If there'd actually been a psycho murderer you'd have already been dead five times over," Angie offered.

"Absolutely, without a doubt. At the time, I was very proud of how I was outsmarting this very slow murderer. Well, Ronnie sees... something on the other side of the glass, he doesn't know what yet, and immediately screams bloody murder. My hair was coming out of my ponytail in chunks so it was sticking out all over and I was covered in mulch and leaves, so it took him a hot second to realize it was just me. He unlocks the door to let me in and by then Chris and April have come running up front. I explain to them that someone is out in the dumpster and that while running for my life I'd locked myself out. April immediately starts to call the cops but Ronnie and Chris decide that no, they'll handle it themselves and make her hang up the phone. So, these dumbasses are armed with the pipe wrench that we used for the plumbing on the soda machine, and a broom. I, dumbass number three, bring up the rear with the mop."

"I would have paid money to watch this," Ryan said.

"I'm sure we looked ridiculous. Anyway, we tiptoe out there and the guys can hear these noises too. Rustling, scratching, crinkling. So, Chris says, 'Hello' and the noises stop. That freaks us out even more.

I'd given Ronnie the key so he unlocks the padlock and Chris is standing there, holding the pipe wrench like a baseball bat, waiting for Ronnie to open the lattice."

"If it was lattice, couldn't you see inside?" Angie asked.

"Well, yeah, if it was daylight, probably, but it was dark as hell back there at night so we couldn't see anything and we didn't have a flashlight. I mean, there was probably one somewhere in the supply closet, but teenagers are dumb panicky animals, right? So, Ronnie unlocks it and starts moving the door out of the way, and Chris steps up, ready to swing. I'm behind Ronnie and we're holding the mop and broom like they're battle spears. I remember it was completely silent except for the wind rattling the dead leaves in the trees.

"Nothing moves. Finally, Ronnie steps forward and uses the handle of the broom to flip open the dumpster lid, and all of the sudden, something in the depths of the dumpster makes this god-awful screeching sound. We see a dark shadow come up out of the dumpster and Chris screams before throwing the wrench at it..."

"Wait, wait. He threw the wrench?" Stacy asked.

"Oh yeah, we had to climb in and search for it the next day because we needed it. Anyway, he misses, and the dumpster demon jumps out and lands on the top of the lattice. All we see is this little striped tail go flying over the edge towards the woods. Before we can even take a breath, a second one, the one that had been skulking around behind the dumpster, probably trying to find a way to spring his compadre from dumpster jail, comes flying out the door past us and bolts up the hillside after its little friend. We all stand there, stunned for like, a full ten seconds before Ronnie starts to laugh. Then, we're all laughing. We'd about lost our shit over some raccoons. Luckily, April hadn't called the cops yet because we would never have lived down the embarrassment."

"Trash pandas," Ryan snorted before finishing his drink. "Jesus."

"Exactly. I had to go home and wash the mulch chunks out of my hair because of a random wildlife encounter. So, anyway, there's my story about the scariest night of my life. Who's up next?"

THE LESSON I NEVER LEARNED

BETH WOLFE

I don't know how to say goodbye and mean it because of all those summer Sunday nights when, after the invitation song was sung and the grown-ups recongregated at the bottom of the church steps and the kids clambered up the sloped side yard to chase lightning bugs and each other, we'd hear fifteen different ways the conversation could have ended but waited until a mom finally said, *we'd better get these kids home and ready for bed*, before we'd head to the car, hoping for a stop at Burger Carte to get hot dogs with chili and slaw and onion rings to eat at my makeshift piano bench table in the living room while *The Jeffersons'* theme song made me crave my piece of the pie long before I even knew what that might mean, where it might lead, or what goodbyes it might require to obtain.

HEART ATLAS

BETH WOLFE

Pretty sure I never traveled
a truly straight road
until the summer of '83,
when my seven-year-old self
sat in the back seat of the new blue Buick
purchased specifically
for that cross-country track.

Dad drove through Kansas,
its tabletop flat land
stretching so far
to the horizon it horrified me.
Because mountain girls
grow up with mountain trails
that go up, down, and all-around

I can ride those roads
without a hint of carsickness.
The thrill of driving,
windows down,
summer breeze carrying
the sound of the cicadas
buzzing and the sweet

scent of honeysuckle.

Those twisty roads are my very veins
carrying my blood to my ventricles.
And while I wasn't nearly as fond
of life's hairpin turns—wishing
my path had remained as straight
as I-70 runs in Kansas, but
you didn't see me careening
over the guardrail—no, sir.

Because a mountain girl knows
how to take those turns,
even the ones that sneak up on you
because some drunk plowed
into the sign that used to warn
of the curve up ahead.

It takes more than trying
to run her off the road
to get her to play it safe.
Maybe she knows
the freedom and power
in taking the twisted road—
as the best views are always
found on the most circuitous,
least travelled, most unexpected
paths, found with your heart
unfolding as your map.

HER

BETSY RAYE ALLEN

You remember when you were twenty-one, fresh out of a relationship that ended not because of a breakup, but because of death. Your significant other had tragically passed away from a medical condition. There were so many long days and endless nights after he passed, remembering the way you felt in his arms, his sweet voice whispering your name in your ear. The way his eyes lit up while talking about your future plans for marriage and what to name your children. Knowing you would never have that with him again was something you couldn't fathom, and you didn't know what to do about the feelings you were trying to process.

A year passed, wallowing in your pain, an endless well that never went dry.

Then you met *her*.

You wrote a story and published it online; she found it. She emailed you, telling you how much she loved it. You were floored. You didn't go to college at the *normal* age and had no formal education. You were a twenty-two-year-old clerk in a big box retail store writing fanfiction about musicians you would never meet. When her words lit up your inbox, you finally felt seen. It was like someone was looking into the hidden parts of your soul, laying them bare, naked, and not being ashamed of it.

"I can't get over your story! The way they meet, the way they fall in love. I feel the emotions. I'm such a fan of yours! I hope you write more."

You wrote her back with fingers that wouldn't stop shaking, thanking her for her words and support. You started writing another story, her words in the back of your mind, encouraging you.

What you didn't expect to happen was for her to email you back. She said she had ideas of stories she wanted to write and wanted your opinion. That opened a floodgate.

You emailed each other constantly, and then it turned into messaging on Instant Messenger. You typed in real-time, for hours at a time, and you couldn't get enough of her. She was like a spring breeze on a warm day that made you feel maybe all could be right with the world.

She was from the Midwest, and attended the University of Notre Dame, where she studied English. You felt *special* that she liked your writing especially because she was an English major who no doubt read much better prose than what you were spewing.

She was Catholic and you were not even close to being a Christian in any sense of the word. You studied Wicca and were proud to be a witchy woman with your crystals and sage and moon water. She was as fascinated by you as you were by her.

Her sweet words through email and instant messaging stayed with you through the day and long into the darkness. It was like she was sunlight, and you were letting her shine into the fog of your grief. You wondered if you could actually be in one of those relationship things again after losing the love of your life. You wondered if you could be in one with a *girl*. You knew you were falling for her.

"I think it's time we take this to the next level. We need to talk on the phone."

With your heart in your throat and the phone to your ear, you dialed the number she had given you. The first time you heard her voice, all husky and breathy, was like magic. You wanted nothing more than to hear that sweet, sexy voice say your name and ask you about your hopes and dreams.

The first phone call lasted three hours, talking about everything and nothing, flirting here and there. You were never good at flirting, but somehow you managed to be witty and subtle with her. When she realized it was midnight, she told you she had to go—she had class early the next morning. With a heavy heart, you said goodbye. She said it wasn't goodbye, it was "talk to you soon."

The phone calls lasted about a week before she broached the subject you had been too fearful to bring up. She wanted you to be her girlfriend, she told you late one Saturday night. She knew you would be perfect together, even if it were long distance, and she asked if you could ever feel the same way about her. You felt your heart jolt, an arrhythmic beat pushing blood through your body once more, restarting your life with the promise of love.

You said yes. You weren't sure how it would work. *If* it would work. But knowing the way you felt about her, there was no way you could say no.

You talked all the time, writing letters and emails. She even came to visit you from Notre Dame one week. It was one of the best weeks of your life, etched forever in your memory. During that week you spent each waking moment with each other; each non-waking moment, too. Your feelings grew deeper than you both realized they could. When she left, a piece of you went with her. Half of your heart was hers.

You would like to tell everyone that twenty-some-odd years later you were still together. You were married. Had the children once promised but never given.

Fate stepped in though, as it always does. You loved her with all your heart, and she loved you, but your brain chemistry had its own plans. Bipolar Disorder hits you with a barrage of emotions, mixed messages, and anger that comes from nowhere with no warning. You didn't know, *you didn't know*, you tell yourself now, but the relationship took a big hit as your brain did what bipolar brains do.

You were irrationally angry that you couldn't be together due to the miles between you. You would argue about her obsession with boybands while you were trying to figure out how to navigate the long distance relationship. You had only been with her for a year and a few months at this point. You were twenty-three when it developed, that mental illness that plagues so many, but you didn't know what it was.

One night you met someone that lived in your city and you hit it off. He was a breath of fresh air. He studied Wicca, too, and you felt a connection with him. Someone that worshipped the god and goddesses, who practiced the craft, drew you in.

You wanted him.

Your brain, the wires crossed and not working together, didn't care about anything except this new input. Love was far away, but this new person was there, in that moment, giving you fresh feelings that would not be denied.

In a manic panic, you called her and broke it off. You'd had your ups and downs before, little tiffs here and there about her fascination with boy bands and how it would sometimes take over her life and you felt like you were in the background.

But, you wanted him so badly that you crushed her heart over the phone. She cried, not understanding what was going on, why you didn't love her anymore. She asked what she did, but you didn't have an answer for her. You thought it was the right decision, to let her go rather than cheat on her. At least that was how the diseased part of your mind rationalized it so you wouldn't feel guilty giving in to pleasure rather than devotion. But there was a part of your brain that begged you not to do it. She had made your heart beat again. Still, you chose to do it, not realizing how bruised and tattered it would still be when you took it from her hands.

And it was all for naught. The relationship you thought you were entering into never happened. It was a glorified one night stand. You knew after it was over that you should have never let her go. You should have stayed with her, even though it was hard to be apart.

It took over ten years for her to speak to you again.

It took Facebook and a Scrabble app to bring you together even tentatively as friends. You had a barely-there relationship. You both would sometimes comment on one another's posts and statuses on Facebook, but that was it.

You longed to have back what you'd lost, but you had burned that bridge so well that the foundations were unstable and couldn't be mended. And in your absence, she had found someone else, someone who loved her, someone she loved. Though you were happy for her, you were sad for yourself. You had lost someone who meant the world to you and could never have them back.

It was in the fall when her wife got in touch with you because she had known what you once meant to each other. She had a tumor in her brain, this woman you both loved. It was bad and she didn't have much time. You sent her one last letter, as you didn't have her phone number and her wife gave you an address. You both had loved to write each other letters, and you prayed to your gods and goddesses that her wife read it to her. It was your explanation as to why you broke it off, that you had a mental illness and she felt the brunt of it, and you were sorry. As you poured out your emotions onto the paper, telling her that you still loved her, that you never stopped, you wondered how she would feel about it.

You like to believe that in her last days she forgave you, that the last thing she remembered about you wasn't your harsh words hurting her so many years ago. You like to believe she still loved you in some deep part of her soul and that forgiveness was overflowing from there. You *want* to believe.

The next time her wife reached out, it was to tell you that the woman you loved had passed away. She was only thirty-six.

Years later and you still think about her, think about how you treated her. You did love her, and you still do, and it has taken you all these years to get over the hurt and shame you carried for so long.

You often sit and wonder how you got where you are, and it's because of her. She gave you the strength to come out of your closet with your family when she got sick. She was so proud when she came out so many years ago, and that helped you be able to come out and live free. Her love was a compass, guiding you through the storm of your identity, her belief in you a constant star in a sky of doubts. The love she shared with you—whether through letters, on the phone, or in person—stayed with you despite the years and miles, and yourself.

And after it all, there you sit alone, knowing you were loved once by her, and it was as pure and sweet as everything you could have ever wanted. Her love was that little light that had shone so brightly in the darkness. But that light is gone, and the shadows begin to crowd around you.

BEATRICE LOUISE

DONALD TOWERS

When we learn about you, it's the evening of
Christmas Day. Now it's May.
You approach, and I so hope
we may, one day, celestially navigate
from our backyard by telescope.
I think, looking up at those beautiful dead lights
that I'm hoping you might
mistake some of their light as mine.
I think my light died out a long time
ago, and I'm too close to create the illusion that I still

shine. Your first mobile came in the mail today
and already I involuntarily imagine it
twirling above my casket.
You're on the way, coming closer as I'm writing this,
but you could as easily be taking your first steps,
starting school, falling in love for the first time,
learning to drive, going off to college,
finding what you love enough to make it your life's work,
falling in love again,
marrying someone you can call your best friend,
having a family, whether that's dogs or kids.

I think about in a few years, when you're starting school,
and suddenly I'm a child who has to take his baby blanket to
kindergarten
with him because it's the thing he's most securely attached to.
I hope it won't be the same for you.

I think about a further future time when I try to give you advice
and you're certain that I don't understand you.
When you assert that I'm ruining your life,
and you go to cry behind your not-quite-slammed door.

I sit at the table in the kitchen, imagining that we're having breakfast.
Like a map of your life, there are lines,
coffee stains, crinkles, and wrinkles drifting into your face.
I'm sorry you got my nose,
but I'm so glad I still get to see you,
that you still want to come home.

A pandemic drove us all inside for quite a while
and during this time I decide to return to school
to pursue a real career that could provide financial stability
for the hypothetical you. And now look at hypothetical you,
here you come.

Planes crash into the Twin Towers,
and from a hotel near the Mayo Clinic
I'm watching the wreckage live on the news
and I wish my own twin-Towers could be here to watch live
as I airplane your food to you.

I'm torn between the past, present, and future—all of time—
all of the time, and I'm never
sure which one is mine.

In the past, I didn't want kids.
I so dearly didn't want them, that it becomes
a running joke between myself and my friends.

But presently? I'm so excited to meet you.
I'm so excited to meet you that in spite of the fact
I'm still thinking of you as some kind of abstract,
the first time I hear your heartbeat,
my hands clap together as I bring them to my mouth
to keep some word or thought or prayer from getting out.

In the future...
I'm sorry I have to leave you.
I promise that I didn't, that I don't, that I will not want to.
Before I do, I hope... so many things.

I'm already losing my sight, and I
know one day I'm going to be blind.
I'm glad you're going to arrive,
that you'll get here before I get there.
Through these dying eyes, though,
I know, I'm gonna try to see beyond sight and life,
through space and time, through the crude eye-
holes gouged in the death mask of Time, I'm
gonna try to catch a glimpse of some future you.

I hope you might see me, too.

FUTURE SHOCK/LOVE POEM

DONALD TOWERS

I.

"I love you."
we fall into
the habit of saying nightly before sleep,
or every time one of us is about to leave,
and, every time you make me laugh in this
certain way that always makes my face hurt,

I say,
"I love you."

Dying is slow; it can take a lifetime.
Death is sudden,
like the way the future always rushes
in, faster than we
thought it would. You're finishing up with dying, and I—
I know the senses go
one at a time. And looking at your living
face this final time—

Always time. I try
to smile for you before your sight goes.

I hold your hand,
press my lips to your lips, to the tip of your nose, your forehead,
because touch is next.
Hearing is supposed to go last.
So, over the blast,
the continuous shrill scream
that means
you're leaving me,
I want to make sure you
know, so,
I say,
"I love you."

II.

I'm planning your funeral,
and I hate knowing how soon you'll
be going underground.
I know you're afraid of the dark— or, you were, and
it breaks my heart a little bit
when the funeral director answers with a laugh
as I ask about a coffin with a night-light in it.

I'm doing my best to honor your wish of having a "FUN-eral."
I try, but don't find myself laughing much anymore.
I try, but don't find myself much in the mirror either;
my face didn't have all these lines
the last time I had to try having fun without
you, the last time I came home
and couldn't tell you how
I wish you'd been there.
How I wish

you were here.
Our living room— now my living room, with you un-living too
soon—
is filled with too many half-inflated balloons, and
that's kind of how it feels living on without you.

Always now, without you.
I descend into mourning, while I
try to deliver your eulogy this morning,
condensing a lifetime of feelings to explain
what you were to me.
What you are to me,
                    still.

Streamers hang as the half-inflated balloons
droop. I droop too, like some sad clown in a suit,
not laughing now. I loathe time as it brings you closer to descending

into the ground.
So, at the wake, with everyone we've loved who is still
around—everyone who I have to love alone now—gathered around,
I say,
"I love you."

III.

We lower you into the ground,
and this has to be the final time life lets me down. (Please.)
I linger here as our kids, their kids, and our friends—all mine now
through this unkind inheritance—threaten to wait for me.
I lie and say, "I'm okay. You go on home,"
and, "I just need some time alone."

When I'm sure everyone else has left,
I lie down on your grave.
I don't know how long hearing hangs on,
but just in case, and for whatever it's worth,
I press my lips to that terrible, turned Earth,
and say,
"I love you,"

"I'm on my way,"
"I'll see you soon,"
"I'll find you,"
"I wish you were here,"
And, I love you.

IV.

I sink down into sleep,
or for once I just find a way not to think
for a while.

I start to claw at the dirt,
digging down, god damn any hurt.
I dig until my fingers start losing some feeling.
Over the fading sound of dirt landing on grass and graves,
my heart beats, pumps blood louder than bombs.
I wonder how long until my other senses might follow,
the same way I'm trying to follow you now.

I wonder if it will be heart or spirit that
will give out on me first. Maybe both,
but it doesn't really matter now as I
dig down
toward you,
and nothing can stop me.
Six feet, give or take;
that's where I meet some kind of fate,
when my hand lands
and makes a
    dull
        dumb
            wooden
                thump.
I pound at what is your front door now,
this coffin, waiting for it to give,
or waiting for you to open up, invite me in.
I get this feeling like, something is trying to slip,
unsure whether that's time or you or everything.
A black hole, or something like it,
opens up above me, pulling.
I am losing me, but it doesn't hurt like losing you.
Sight, taste, smell, and touch
begin their rush out of me.

Going the way everything will, eventually.
If I could speak—
I don't think it'd matter much,
but the pull from that black hole starts to give,
then it goes altogether.
The lid goes next.
Sense and feeling flood back inside,
as I'm blown from out of your grave;
dirt and wood chips flying alongside me.
Crash landing, happy crying.
I reach down and out,
to you.

Fickle fingers keep failing to find hold
a sick, cold burst emerges from another Vantablack Hole,
but finally— fingers find purchase, pulling.
Hands meeting, grabbing, holding
straining against the dark, cold
pull of the nothing that devours.

My bony legs stick up out of your grave
like unfortunate flowers,
and I love you.

You—my little anchor holding me down,
pulling me now, under the ground,
and in, and back to you.
We're tidal locked, my moon.
I wish I could see you one more time,
but this is just fine, too.
I'm home again, just in time;
your hearing finally gives
out and so does mine,
and I love you.

CPR

FRANCES ADAM

You tear me open. My guts are hot –
    they send off tendrils of steam to rise in the black air.
    Grab,

                        twist,

                                        dig in,

    bury your fingers in my organs, sifting
    "What are you looking for?" I ask,

                        and you smile
    you push aside loops of bowel and peek under a kidney,
    "You shouldn't feel much, just a pinch," you say,
    wrist-deep now,

                                    eyes cast skyward
    as you chew the inside of your cheek
    (that's the face you make when you're concentrating — I know it
well)
    Your fingers are soft and strong as they search for an edge and
    I relish the feeling, though I hate to admit it.
    "I don't have all night," I say,
    as you find your grip and pull,
    my diaphragm peeling back like the foil on a new jar of peanut
butter
    "Not much longer now,"
    you reassure me, even at this moment.

You reach up,   up
your knuckles bump my sternum from the wrong side
I want to say, "It was more than a pinch"
I want to say, "Same time next week?" but
with my chest flayed open and your hands in my lungs,
words fail me.
I close my eyes and smile,
and when you bring your lips to mine,
when you squeeze my heart,
I can't tell if it's resuscitation

                                          or goodbye.

THE WOODS

FRANCES ADAM

I went to the woods to look for you
but they had changed. Plants had died and grown.
I went to the woods to look for you,
but all I found was your ghost,
running on the soft earth between the pines.
I went to the woods to look for you
and walked all our old paths
but when I went to the woods to look for you,
I knew you wouldn't be there.
I went to the woods to look for you,
and I couldn't find you so I left you there,
in pieces and crumbs. The wind blew and carried you.
I went to the woods to look for you.

FAIRY TALES

GABRIELLE GILLIAM

I'd love to be as confident
when it comes to what I want
as Goldilocks in a stranger's house.

I want to know which chair will feel
just right so I don't lose circulation
in my feet and my ass doesn't fall asleep.

And which bed holds the mystical balance
between firm and soft while staying cool
enough to keep night sweats at bay.

And which of the bears I face
will be sweet enough to join me at the table
instead of chasing me down
because they'd like to swallow me whole.

I NEED TO STOP FALLING IN LOVE WITH FICTIONAL MEN

GABRIELLE GILLIAM

But even their flaws are perfect,
just broken enough that love can fix them
and we all want a project. I could
name drop here, but the list would fill
its own book and we all have a different notion
of perfect. You know which ones
would fill your own pages, but I will say
that not all of mine are vampires
(though a few might be)
and not all are wealthy English men
who own half of Derbyshire
(though one might be)
and my heart is so filled with paper men
it's a miracle I'm not covered in paper cuts.

A SILENCE

GABRIELLE GILLIAM

Such a small thing,
a pause between breaths
yet yours can fill this car

be carried in your pocket
as you walk five steps ahead

drag across the sand leaving
long tracks like an alligator's tail
down to the crashing surf

an expansive horizon
of holding your tongue

BEAUTIFUL NOW

HEATHER NOBLE

She thought it would have more fanfare, maybe a cake
And someone would hand off a large manila envelope, crisp and
golden,
marked 'adult.'
Maybe marked top secret
Maybe on a Monday at 8:00 a.m., when things should start
like diets and new jobs.

She would start to think differently.
Be serious a lot.
The envelope would hold keys to a house,
a practical car with heated seats
and she'd have a practical wardrobe
in shades of cream and gray and blue.
Constructed of things you iron,
and things you button,
things with darts.

And you'd know how many minutes to boil an egg
Where to get your pants hemmed
what compound interest means.
Everything, she thought,
Would be cool and clear and calm

like beige beach sand
like white
Zen garden sand
sliding her fingers through it, like tines on a rake

But,
none of that happened.

A tropical depression began somewhere
between last baby tooth and first driver's license.
It started to rain, soft at first, but soaking
There were boys; then *THAT* boy, then a wedding
one baby, then another; it rained harder, the earth turned plastic
feet churned the mud, but she held on
To the children, to the trees, to the boy-turned-man.

Lilly of the valley pushed through the grass, the moss,
Like white stars against the night,
intoxicating the damp with sweet.
Sometimes things made sense and the sun dappled them
    yellow and white
But mostly rain fell; bottle green, blue and teal
The children swam,
she held on--fingers dovetailed against the tug of current
Rain, at times, created a common enemy
And they huddled inside, warm and dry, full of plots
and plans, and slept in each other's arms
    feeling understood.
The baby, the toddler, the woman, the man
Like petals of a rose, arms and graceful fingers curving,
velvet and heavy with sleep

At midnight,
things make perfect sense.

she awoke, with a jolt of clarity-
    She'd dreamt of time wasted
    making lists of things she didn't have.
If only she'd seen these moments in
her life exactly as they are. And not through
the critical lens of others
if only she'd
giver her pride leave to
linger in it, the lovely sounds of sleeping children
Lashes and cheeks outlined opal from the
lavender moon
    parting the curtain of rain.

She sees reluctant beauty in their old house, now.
Toeing a silent pattern down the creaking hall,
    She goes to him
The ache of this beautiful life, plothering down
The ache of imperfection, of appreciation
fills the vault of her mouth.
—as she wakes him with a kiss.

Rain sluices rivulets down the picture window.
Drumming rain
  rocks the children deep in dreams.
Shushing rain
  hides stuttered words, fragments
uttered, while They eschew the bed, with its telling box spring
and make love on the carpet, in the next room,
in the dark,
    and always, always, in the rain.

In the breathing dark
they settle; big spoon, little spoon.
She found his hands, wound his fingers
with hers like fiddle head ferns in spring.
    And, though they were warned not to plant them-
from the leafy earth grew morning glories, wild from rain
in colors they had almost forgotten; magenta, bluebird blue,

the purple of kings.
And those vines, well-watered, green and eager, wove tendrils
wrapped the old house
with its white paint chipping, its mossy roof
—and they liked it all the more—
This random
Unplanned, beautiful now.

FACADE

HEATHER NOBLE

With all the razzamatazz on the vids about the new makeup palette, Facade, you can bet I was frantic to get it. Needed it, in fact.

I mean did you see on all the vids how the model's skin glowed? That wasn't CGI, I scoped it—her skin had *no* lines at all. And she was knockin' three decades at a guess. It was perfect like baby's skin. Well, like maybe a one-monther, when they've fed up and puffed out some with those healthy cherub cheeks. That's where the word cheruby comes from, after all, isn't it?

Yeah, I've seen a baby. A cousin brought one over. All puffy like a marshmallow but heavy as an anchor, I tell you. They plopped it in my lap and had a good laugh at the face I was making, I suppose, because the baby started crying. And the smell! Not endearing. At all. They took the baby back and I asked if they were always so fat and you know my mom got jacked calling me rude and making apologies. Cousin bursts out crying saying she thinks the Synthamil formula mix vid is wrong about the baby's hunger cry. She thinks it just wants held. Hot, sweaty, leachy, shite-smelling thing wants held all the time? Getting my tubes knotted now I tell you.

My mom says I'm spoiled because I'm still the baby in this house and the look she gives me is half mean, half prideful, I swear. I don't say anything, cause really anything I add will just jack everyone up, so I just slump in the chair and take the hit. Everyone is so touchy nowadayz.

No wonder there's so many trollz on the webs.

And, maybe I *am* obsessed. But I know what I want: Facade!

To create a buzzbuzz on the pre-release, the UWANIT site was having a fan giveaway. Oh, Yeah! I'd be among the first to sample the palette, named *Tahiti Robot*. There's an AD to watch and a quiz. Always a friggin' AD! There'll be ADs to watch at the Pearly Gates, I bet! So, I set up the

Adskimmer to knockout that problem, and I programed my housebot to spam entries at a reasonable pace to win, but not flag us. Keep a low profile. And I won!

Facade is worth all the buzzbuzz. My skin is cheruby, I tell you. Dreamy. I'm tellin' everyone! They're number one in sales now. Added a Facade moisturizer, tinted and non, that's catching on with parents and even the fossils my great Greatie's age, can u believe?

Except *my* Greatie—she won't touch it.

I tell her it's fab, I feel so chilled. I just run my hand over my cheruby forehead and cheeks. Feel so content sometimes it's kinda weird, like I've gone all peacelovewoodstock.

They must be marketing geniuses, because now that the razzamatazz has spread, they added men's aftershave and lotion. Shampoo and conditioner. Even baby lotion. And dropped the price.

Accessible to all, chirps the AD.

Now everyone uses it except a few holdouts that don't know what they're missing. Now they offer *incentives* to use the product, can u believe? They have a lotto, too. Salesbots ping your phone all the time. I've won stuff nightly. Not much challenge, I tell you. Pretense to passing it out, I say.

But I like the feeling I get. I use several products now. Twice or more a day.

I went to visit my Greatie at the Pasture house. She's got a pile of unused Fasade stuff in a ratty 'ol basket. She's a holdout. I sorta admire her though I don't get her at all. I like her fab stories, though. She knows *lots* of history cause' she used to teach. Her stories are *way* better than the boring vids at school. She tells me did you know American Indians used boiled bear fat for lotion and for their hair? Can you imagine how that *stank*? Especially crowded in a teepee over a fire? No thank you. She laughs at the face I'm makin', cause she likes grossing me out. Her wrinkled fossil cheeks pull into a grin like a set of crinkly curtains.

I nudge her pile of unused product and I tell her they say the lotion is supposed to be mood lifting. (Like we hadn't figured *that* out!) Greatie says she wouldn't put it past the gov to pump it full of meds an' stuff to keep everyone a little sheepy.

Without thinkin', I get jacked, defensive, straight off. I start talking and in a minute or so she interrupts me, and asks if I remember her favorite Socrates quote?

"The unexamined life isn't worth living," I chirp right off, cause she's said it so friggin' much.

She nods like I've said something more than just that. I try again to tell her Facade makes quality products, it's certified non gen mod, vegan, classified organic... I mean, you can *practically* eat it. And she said you know hemlock and foxglove are organic too but they can kill you just as dead, unless you know what you're doing, kiddo. She leans back in her chair and gives me that long look of hers, points her chin at the stack, says, "but maybe they know exactly what they're doing. What do you think?"

Ridin' the Tran back home, I suddenly realize how chill the other riders are. No buskers or ranters on the Tran for a while now. Extra quiet. And, even though I feel the mellow of Facade oozing like flavorless honey into my elbows and knees, what she said repeats.

I tell you, she always says stuff that sticks to me like hot gum on a flip flop.

THE DIARY OF A TRANSGENDER TEEN

JAXX MORGAN

December 2nd

~~*Dear Diary,*~~
No, that's gross. Should I name it?
~~*Dear Bob,*~~
Maybe I shouldn't be doing this.
~~*To Whom It May Concern:*~~
That's very professional.
To Me, To Future Me,
Who else would I be writing for?
That's cliché. Who cares?
Intros are for losers anyway.

Today was classic, filled to the brim with drama that you knew was happening or about to happen. A catfight breaks out over a cigarette. National Guard recruiters challenge the football team to do a shit ton of pushups in two minutes, hoping to buy a bunch of broke but athletic white boys, with the promise of a free college experience. My best friend cheats on her boyfriend with a new guy and then tells me that they're cousins when I ask about it. Personally, I've never loved my cousins enough to shove my tongue down their throats, but that's "Sweet Home Alabama," for you. Well, except for the fact that we live in Kentucky, but does that matter?

Hailey and I were often known as "The Double Trouble Couple," considering we shared the same first name—different spellings, of course—and we were essentially the baddest bitches and chaos-causers in the ninth grade. Or, that's what Hailey said. Did I believe her? Not really.

Hailey was the drama queen. The kid who picked fights to determine the social hierarchy—the skinny, rich, popular girls never stood a chance. She's the girl who wouldn't back down from a fight to save her life. She always said it was better to get your ass kicked rather than refuse like a coward. She was a fool like that—a fool that I couldn't get enough of.

I, on the other hand, was the complete opposite. Well, sort of. I used to fight, but not anymore—I had a full-ride athletic scholarship and didn't want to lose it because of a "discipline" issue. No, my new thing was making people feel inferior when I spouted what I believed to be larger words—most of which I found searching for synonyms of smaller words. It turns out that fallacious doesn't mean bad. It means something based on false beliefs, but it didn't stop me from describing horrendous school lunches as such. It was fine though. No one in my high school knew what the word meant. And Hailey never failed to remind me that I was the "smartest" kid in the school. Did I believe her? I wanted to.

Today's classic feel was broken when Emma—who was basically a small-town celebrity—passed me a handwritten note during biology. I glanced hesitantly at the teacher before accepting it. I unfolded it.

Didn't know you were a tranny

I looked at her with a confused expression. My eyebrows were knitted together and my head had tilted slightly to the left, like a dog hearing its name for the first time. She just smiled at me. I felt like I had missed the joke. I scribbled:

A what?

She opened it as soon as she received it. I glanced up at our teacher. How had she not noticed us passing notes? I fidgeted with the zipper on my jacket anxiously as she wrote.

Ask your girlfriend :)

I didn't want to ask Hailey. I didn't know what the word meant and I knew almost every word. Sort of. But that was irrelevant. Hailey was a drama queen, yes, but gossip? Never. Why would she tell Emma, of all people, something that wasn't…probably wasn't true? I folded the note up neatly and shoved it into my back pocket.

I found her during the evening break in the restroom and I pushed the note into her hand.

"What's this?"

"Explain."

She opened the folded paper gently and read it quietly. "It's nothing," she said, placing the note on the sink before trying to slip around me. I stepped in front of her and shoved her backward. She gently bumped into the wall behind her.

As another group of girls entered the restroom, I stepped closer to her, hoping to avoid being overheard and hoping Emma wouldn't notice I was following her orders. "What. Does. It. Mean?" I was close enough to smell the garlic from today's lunch on her breath.

"Hmm," she said. "I don't think I've seen this side of you before. You know, if you wanna go full dom, you should put both of your hands on the wall so you can pin me."

"What? What are you talking about? I'm not—"

Hailey laughed. It was a soft, deep sound that was contagious 90% of the time.

"Marsh, I'm serious," I said, stepping away from her. I had nicknamed her Marsh when we were little and she had told me that she hated her name because it was too common. I had asked her for her preferred name, but she said she didn't have one. I told her that if she didn't come up with one, I'd call her "Marshmallow." Marsh was just simpler.

"It's just Emma trying to cause trouble," she said with a sigh. She pushed an umber strand of hair out of my eyes. "But, hey, isn't that us? We're trouble? I mean, how many queers do you see overthrowing the patriarchy in this neck of the woods? We're trouble and no one can change that."

I nodded and she kissed me gently.

"But..."

She sighed again.

"What does it mean? I won't let it bother me. I just, you know, want to know."

The bell rang, signaling that our break was over. Hailey kissed my forehead as she grabbed the paper off the sink. She crumpled it into a ball and pitched it into the trash can. "It means I love you no matter what."

Did I believe her? Yeah.

December 3rd

Dear Internet:
I hate you.

I had the stupidity to look "tranny" up on the internet, but now I'm even more confused. What's a transvestite? Cross-dresser? Transsexual? I didn't really dress like a man, did I? I didn't feel like I did. I mean, I just wore casual band t-shirts and ripped skinny jeans. That's basically every ordinary girl in the school. It's not like I wore those Laker jerseys with red basketball shorts and country boots. And I definitely didn't walk around with a Mountain Dew bottle to spit tobacco juice in. That's just nasty.

I went on a spiral after that. Is Hailey actually gay or does she only like me because she thinks I'm a guy? I mean, she always said she didn't hate men; she was just disgusted by the sight of dicks. Am I the best of both worlds? No, no, I can't be. I'm not a guy. I mean, I never wore makeup or painted my nails, but that's just refusing a societal standard. You can be a girl without wanting that stuff. I'm not a guy.

Of course, I did the best thing I could do considering the circumstances. I looked for "Am I Trans?" quizzes on Quotev. I had very mixed results. Most of them were like: did you play with cars or dolls, do you like makeup, do you wish you were the other gender, and how much do you hate yourself? Some said, "You're trans!" Others said, "Oh no, you're trans." Some quiz results seemed relieved when I passed as "cis," whatever that means. Confusion was the worst and it was giving me a headache. I just needed some reassurance. That's it. Just reassurance. I texted Hailey.

Hey. I just have to know.
Do you only love me
because you think I'm
a dickless boy?

December 19th

Dear Santa,
My only wish this year
is that my brain
will be thoughtless
and my spirits high.
I guess that's two wishes.

Winter break had finally arrived and I had made plans to do everything I possibly could do to avoid my thoughts, which turned out to be pretty hard.

"Josh, keep your fingers out of the outlet!"
Would they still let me babysit if they knew I was a guy?
Well, they thought I was a guy.

"Welcome to Good Samaritan Food Pantry!"
Would I be allowed to volunteer here if I was a guy?
I don't think being trans is very Christian-like.

Despite all my efforts to stay busy, nothing could distract me at night. When everyone else was supposed to be sleeping, I tossed and turned. I got up and I paced. I wrote stupid journal entries and poems and trashed them later. I thought about it, running the idea of being trans through my head over and over again until I thought my brain would explode. If all things that are typically gendered are just societal standards and expectations, then what is gender? Well, if we look at things scientifically, there's no such thing as a chosen gender. Or maybe your chosen gender is just how you choose to express yourself. That's why they call it cross-dressing. Maybe it's all about style. And there's only one way to find out. And that, my friends, is how I ended up with a bowl cut.

January 3rd

Dear Future Me:
Promise me you'll go
to a stylist next time.

Though my hair had grown out a little bit, it was still massively uneven. My parents were furious. My mom wanted to even it out but my dad convinced her the only way to even it out was to shave it. I couldn't go to school like that. I couldn't. I wouldn't. And then I did.

I texted Owen, my friend, and the only other high schooler on my bus, and told them about the situation. When I stepped on the bus, Owen grimaced and then waved me toward the seat at the very back of the bus. I sat down and they unzipped their backpack. Inside was a very white wig.

"What's that?"

"It's a wig. I was going to use it for my Ken Kaneki cosplay. You know, from Tokyo Ghoul? But I thought you might need it more right now and it's a long way until Halloween anyway."

"I have brown hair though."

"Just tell everyone you dyed it. You just wanted to switch it up."

"Everyone will think Hailey broke up with me and I had a mental breakdown."

"You're not that kind of girl."

"I'm not a—" I cleared my throat. "How do I put it on?"

As one could guess, no one thought I was cool and no one thought I had a mental breakdown. Everyone thought I was crazy for wearing a greasy white wig that smelled like cigarette smoke. And perfume. Well, perfume just made it that much more overwhelming for the few people who wanted to be seen near me.

And of course, the rumors flew. Some said I had cancer and had lost all of my hair. Some said that I was just looking for attention. Others proclaimed I had an identity crisis and I was trying to mirror Emma, who had recently gone from wheat-yellow hair to platinum blonde. It would grow back out. I just had to keep telling myself that.

March 10th

Dear Future Me,
The trans support group
said being trans is okay
and we should embrace it.

I joined a support group called "Kentuckiana Trans." I stumbled across their abandoned Facebook page during a Google search, and I hopelessly reached out to the admin, Teresa, and she instantly invited me to a Discord chat/group. Honestly, the app is super confusing, but I'll learn.

Multiple people in the group are non-binary. Basically, they exist outside the gender spectrum, which is hard for me to understand, since everyone seems to view gender differently. So many people support that too. It's like they don't need a concrete definition because gender is different for everyone. It's weird, but it's also freeing. Chaotic but free.

"Do you have a preferred name?" Teresa asked for the hundredth time at the end of our weekly video meeting. She would ask me at least once a week about it. In the past, I had always told her "no."

"Am I supposed to?"

"No. A lot of people don't change their names. I just want to keep checking in because I know you're new to this and I want to make sure you're comfortable enough to tell us if anything changes."

"What would I change it to?"

Teresa shrugged. "Whatever you'd like. If you want to explore, baby name generators online are a great place to start."

One week later, everyone is calling me Nicholas.

March 27th

Dear Marsh,
I changed my name.

Nicholas didn't work out like I had hoped, but I had found something better, something that sounded like me. Haydn Nicholas Newvonne had a nice ring to it. But now, I had to reintroduce myself to the world. Baby steps though.

I tried to figure out how to tell my girlfriend. She knew. She had been reassuring me so much over the last few months. She loved me. That was simply the facts. But she deserved to hear the story from me. I deserved to hear it, to find a way to say it. So I sent her a poem, the first one that made me feel alive.

<u>The History of a Name</u>

Haydn.
Five letters.
Three the same,
Mostly, just rearranged.
He was the boy
that I created when I was nine.
A character with fire hands
and a genuine smile.
He was the boyfriend
that I created when I was thirteen.
A fake to make me feel
that I belonged to something.
He was the music
that I copied when I was fourteen.
A determined pianist
from the 18th century.
He was the shy boy
that I revealed when I was 15.

A spider-obsessed lad
with a story worth sharing.
He was always there
that boy that became me.
A difficult story destined
to have a happy ending.

CHORD CHANGE

JD BYRNE

Kluvier took another slow sip while he stared down his server. She'd already circulated, twice, to ask if she could get him anything else. The truth was that he couldn't afford anything else. It hadn't been a bad day on Claxton Green, but when Valnu came to collect on Kluvier's back debt it hadn't left him with much. He'd hoped to have enough for dinner, at least, but he could only afford one drink at Cafe Birrim, the cheapest place on the promenade. At least they gave you free zahl clusters. It would have to be supper for tonight.

The server caught his eye, wavered for a moment, then walked on. He had at least another few minutes to enjoy the cool evening air as he watched denizens of Neska walk back and forth, on their way to dinner or a play or perhaps something more private.

At his feet, Braax chittered and slashed at the bars of his cage.

"I know, buddy, but it's not my fault they won't let you out," Kluvier said, trying to calm the little, black, furry goblin. "Not too much longer." He'd need to feed Braax, too, after the little beast's hard day at work powering the bellows of his organ.

The organ sat on the table across from Kluvier. It was battered and worn, with chunks of wood missing from the body, but the keyboard was in pristine condition and allowed him to play with what he thought was a feel and sense of control that surpassed the typical street musician. It was his livelihood, after all.

Braax calmed down, as much as the little goblin ever did, and

Kluvier took another drink. He closed his eyes and savored the sweet spiced flavor, followed by the kick of alcohol on the back end.

"Is that yours?"

Kluvier opened his eyes. A woman in her mid to late 20s was standing on the promenade, on the other side of the chain that marked the boundary of the cafe. She was wearing light blue robes that signaled she was an acolyte from one of the city's numerous cults. His mind couldn't summon up just what sect claimed those colors. "I'm sorry?"

"That?" she said, pointing to the organ. "Is it yours?"

He nodded.

"You play it, then?"

"Every day," he said. It wasn't unusual for passersby to stop and admire the instrument. "Can I help you?"

"Actually, could I sit down a minute?" She nodded toward the open chair next to him.

He could see weariness in her eyes, in the way she didn't quite hold herself completely upright. "Sure."

She climbed over the chain, nearly falling as her robes got tangled in it. When she finally managed to sit down, it was with an audible sigh. "Are you playing here tonight?"

Kluvier laughed. "Oh no. The city elders decided long before I was born that having a goblin out of its cage indoors was a bad idea. Not that Braax here would ever be any trouble."

The young woman looked under the table at the small cage. The tiny beast whirled inside its confines and slobbered at the bars. She sat back up. "You need the goblin?"

"No goblin, no music," he said, patting the collapsed bellows on the side of the organ. "So I'm limited to playing outside, usually over at Claxton Green." He nodded up the street. "I'm sure they've got someone with a lute or a pan pipe or something in there tonight, though, if that's what you're after."

She sat for a moment, as if gathering herself. Then she sat up straight and presented her open palms to him. "I apologize for my lack of manners. I am Shyana."

"Of course," Kluvier said, nodding toward the robes. "I should have known. I'm Kluvier." He returned the open palmed gesture.

"Actually, Kluvier, what I'm after is someone like you, I think," she said. "I'm not in need of music generally as much as someone who can make a certain kind of it."

"What kind is that?"

"The kind with," she paused, putting her head in one hand, as if thinking. "Oh, what's it called when you can play many notes at once?"

"Polyphony," he said. "Yeah, most musicians you'd find in a place like this can't do that kind of thing very well. This," he patted the organ, "would definitely do it." Images flashed through his head of playing in some kind of religious ceremony. Didn't matter that he didn't believe any of it, so long as the coin was right. "You want to hire me?"

"Well, not exactly hire," she said, then moved on. "How heavy is that? You carry it around?"

"On my back, yeah," he said, making a note to get back to the money. "It's a haul, believe me, between home in South Luffop and the green."

"But you're used to carrying it around, long distance?"

"I suppose," he said, "look I . . ."

"And how many notes can it play?"

That was a question he'd never gotten before. It took him a moment. "I suppose you could mash every key down at the same time if you wanted, but I'm not sure how long Braax could keep the bellows going at that rate. Regardless," he held up his hands, "I've only got ten fingers. That's the best I can do."

"That would be enough," she said, like she was ticking off a checklist in her head. "Can you make up the music as you go along? Improvise?"

"Of course," he said, with more confidence than deserved. He had no formal training and couldn't hope to keep up with someone like his friend Andra, who played recitals on the big organ at the Great Library. But he could muddle through just about anything and that was surely good enough.

It was time to come back around to the most important topic of discussion. "Shyana, you want me to play somewhere?"

She nodded.

"Then that's going to cost you. This," he pointed to the instrument, "is how I make a living. And I've got two mouths to feed."

As if on cue, Braax snarled and chittered beneath the table.

Shyana swallowed hard. "How much?"

He fought back a smile. He didn't actually do paid performances, so he was going to have to figure out how to make the most money without overshooting. "Where would this performance be?"

She looked across the promenade and pointed to the mountains that rose behind the city.

"In the Singing Hills?" His back already ached. "Outdoors, I'm guessing? Not a problem, obviously, but it affects my fee."

"Yes," she said.

"What kind of audience?"

She thought for a moment. "I'm not really sure. Small, regardless, only a few would be listening."

That was a little disappointing, but the logistics were going to be costly, regardless. "And when?"

"Soon," she said, eager. "As soon as you can. It's quite urgent."

"Urgent." He wasn't going to try and figure out what was so urgent that it required a street organ performance.

"Everything may depend on it," she said, then added, more quietly, "or not."

Kluvier had no idea where she was going, so he decided he would price himself out of the market. Whatever Shyana wanted, he was certain someone else would be happy to oblige for less coin. "Well, if that's the case. My normal rate for a performance is fifty coins." He thought that sounded like a reasonable, but attainable, number. "For what you're suggesting, with the quick turnaround and hiking up in the hills, I'm afraid I couldn't go any lower than one fifty."

She looked at him, eyes moist. "One hundred and fifty coins? I don't have that. One in my order doesn't collect wealth, you know."

Kluvier felt sorry for her but wasn't about to show it. "Like I said, I do have to make a living."

"If I can't find someone to help me, making a living will be the least of our worries," she said, crossing her arms and staring at the table.

He picked over her words carefully. She said "our worries," not "his" or "yours." It wasn't a threat, but a statement of belief. And it was getting to him. He leaned down, under the table to check on Braax, who he could at least use to talk things out. Naturally, the furry little monster had picked this moment for his evening nap. He lay in his cage, tongue hanging out the side of his mouth and drooling.

Before his good sense could stop him, Kluvier sat up and said, "look, this clearly means a lot to you. I can knock it down to one twenty-five, but that's really the best I can do."

Shyana wiped her cheek with the back of her robed arm. "One hundred twenty-five?"

He nodded. "If you can come up with that in a couple of days, I'll do it. You can find me on the green, any day of the week."

Shyana sat up, took a deep breath, then stood. She held out her palms and bowed slightly. "Thank you, Kluvier. I hope to see you in the next few days." She walked away without saying anything else.

Kluvier sat for a moment, stunned that he'd agree to her proposal. Then he downed the rest of his drink and plucked Braax and his cage up off the ground and put it on the table in front of him. The little goblin awoke and started snarling and snapping. "I'm not sure we'll ever see her again, buddy, but if we do I suspect we'll be sorry."

~

Claxton Green was the center of public life in Neska. The tight, winding streets along the river were where the city had first sprouted, but it was here that the prosperous, peaceful city expressed itself the most. It was the place where visitors from around Hubrul would come and wander, open mouthed, at the opulence.

At the north end was the Great Library, a center of knowledge and learning renowned across Hubrul. Kluvier had only been in the actual library once, in search of a book on the care of goblins when he first got Braax. It wasn't that he didn't read or wanted to remain ignorant of the wider world. The library, with its marble pillars, its wide, sweeping staircases, and the shelves of books and scrolls that seemed to stretch to the horizon, was intimidating. He wasn't ashamed to admit that. He really only went there when Andra gave a recital on the library's massive pipe organ and then it was right to the recital hall.

At the south end of the green was the ancient amphitheater, where actors and musicians had performed for generations. Kluvier thought the closest he'd ever get to playing there was to walk slowly by with his organ on his back. It was a beautiful symbol of what art could be, even if it was out of the grasp of a street musician like himself. Behind the amphitheater, the Singing Hills rose in a massive echo of the amphitheater shell itself.

Between them was a wide, rolling lawn that was crisscrossed by paths. Sculpture and fountains dotted the landscape. Along either side, across brick-paved promenades, were numerous cafes, shops and galleries. The green was a destination, a place to spend a day and lose track of time. Carts selling food and drink appeared frequently. In other words, it was the perfect place for someone like Kluvier to set up and try to make a living.

Kluvier had a few different spots on the green where he liked to set up. Some were along heavily trafficked paths and people walked by all day. Others were where people would congregate, stopping to enjoy a snack or admire some fixture of the green. Today he picked one of those places, a clutch of trees across from the bronze statue of Duhda, a mythical hero of Neskan legend. It was both a destination for some people and a handy landmark and meeting place for others. There was always traffic and people generally seemed to appreciate his presence.

Not that they always showed it. Kluvier told himself that his relationship with an audience was more pure than Andra's, who only played for people who had already paid for the privilege of hearing her. Kluvier put the product out there and let people decide what it was worth, if anything. Some days only a few coins wound up in his box, but he knew those were well earned. Over the years he'd had plenty of practice not scowling at those who would stop, listen, then walk away without contributing to his wellbeing.

He took Braax from his cage and looped his leash around the nearest tree. That was more for show than out of any real need, as Braax and Kluvier had been together for eight years and the fluffy ball of aggression wasn't going to run off. His very being could frighten people, although Kluvier had never seen him go after a person. Nonetheless, part of his job was putting the public at ease and if that meant providing additional assurance that Braax wouldn't go berserk and cause mayhem, so be it.

Kluvier had purchased the organ from a retiring colleague years ago. It was always meant to be a first instrument, something he could earn money with to invest into something more modern, more powerful. Instead, it kept a constant stream of coin just to keep things in working order. Last summer he'd needed an entirely new keyboard, which had almost caused him to give up altogether. He couldn't stand the thought of doing real work, however, and wouldn't let himself be drawn away from the music.

If not powerful or a work of art, at least the organ was robust. It was designed to be portable, as these things go, with compartments for storing legs that helped the organ stand at the proper height for Kluvier to play it. The turnwheel on which Braax ran to power the bellows folded out from one side. Kluvier had everything set up and ready to play in less than twenty minutes, which was about as fast as it could be done.

Kluvier retrieved Braax, who had been lounging in the shady grass, and swapped his regular leash for the harness that held him in place on the turnwheel. "Ready go to work, buddy?"

The slavering beast grinned and started to walk, then jog, finding the pace that would let him keep going for a while keeping the bellows full.

While Braax got up to speed, Kluvier got out the collection box. It was plain brown wood, but sturdy, with a hinged lid at the top. On the inside was a sign that read "Kluvier and Braax appreciate your support and enthusiasm!"

Over the years, Kluvier had built up a repertoire of dozens of songs, from folk songs to cult hymns and chants. He would never be able to play with Andra's finesse, but he had the ability to hear a song a few times, play it once, and then forever be able to retrieve it.

His first hour was always the same, a way to warm himself up and to gauge his audience. Some days the more modern, popular music was what people wanted. Other times the long, slow chords of cult hymns that had soaked into wider culture of the years provided the perfect background. Once that was out of the way, and Braax had his first break of the day, Kluvier would let his fingers wander, dipping in and out of known songs while taking tangents of variations on themes. During another break he heard a woman pass by whistling an odd-metered tune he'd never heard before. He worked on it, and several variations, for most of the next hour.

The predicted rain held off, which kept the traffic consistent. The coins dropping into the box were few and far between, but as the sun started fall behind the Great Library they at least started to clink against each other nicely when a new one was thrown in.

Kluvier let Braax off his turnwheel to attack a small bowl of water while he knelt and started counting the coin. He hoped to get everything counted and packed away before Valnu showed up to take his cut again. Kluvier was just about done when a human-shaped shadow fell across the box. Kluvier cursed under his breath, then a bag of coin thudded to the ground beside the box. He looked up.

"Is that enough?" It was Shyana. She was breathing hard and her robes, which had been so well put together yesterday, were dirty and mussed. There was a bruise starting to blossom under her left eye.

"What happened to you?" Kluvier grabbed the bag and stood.

"I did what I had to," she said. "Is that enough?"

Kluvier hefted the bag in his hand. He tried to remember the details of their conversation last night, what price he'd settled on. What he was holding had to be enough, given the lengths she apparently went to get it. "Yeah, it'll do. Are you all right?"

She wiped sweat and dirt away from her forehead with her sleeve, further soiling it. "I will be, if that's enough."

He nodded affirmatively. "Yeah, yeah. When do you want me to play?"

"How about now?" Shyana said, bending over, hands on knees.

"Now?" Kluvier certainly didn't remember her saying the gig was tonight.

She stood up and took a couple of deep breaths. "If not tonight, it may be too late."

"Too late?"

"I'll explain on the way," she said, "I promise."

Kluvier looked at the bag of coin. Without pouring it out on the ground he couldn't be sure how much was in it, but it was more than a day's wages. And for a brief performance? He couldn't afford not to humor her. "All right," he said, tying the bag to his belt. He nodded at Braax. "Keep an eye on him while I pack up, OK?"

Shyana glanced at Braax, who did that kind of jittering, frightening dance that he did when he was meeting a new friend.

⌇

The Singing Hills curved around Neska almost like a natural amphitheater. Kapusshaw Peak was the largest of the six, its highest point just clearing the others by a few dozen feet. Numerous paths led up into the hills, and to the top of Kapusshaw. Kluvier didn't consider himself much of a mountaineer, but he'd explored the hills before, although he'd never been to the top of any of them. The path they were on wasn't any of the ones he could remember.

Shyana led the way. She had strapped a contraption on her back that held a torch out to her right, lighting their path. Braax followed, off his leash and darting here and there, exploring the rocks and shrubs alongside the path. Kluvier came last, the weight of the organ on his back compounding with every step.

So far the explanation Shyana had promised hadn't arrived. Kluvier decided he couldn't make it much further until it did. "I need a break," he said, stopping and putting the organ down. He leaned against a large rock that stood next to the path.

Shyana whirled around. "No, we have to keep going!"

Braax bounded into the path and yapped at her, teeth bared.

"I was on my feet, working, all day," Kluvier said. "I need a rest. And, before we climb any further up this mountain, you need to tell me what we're doing out here." They hadn't seen another soul since they started going up, which Kluvier suspected wasn't a coincidence.

Shyana hung her head, apparently resigned to the fact that she needed him. She walked back to where he stood, ignoring Braax as she passed by. She put the torch-harness down and smoothed out her robes. "What do you think these mean?"

"I know you're an acolyte of some kind," he said, "but I never really knew what the various colors meant. Is that what this is about?"

She held out one arm, the loose blue sleeve drooping. "Light blue, the color of the sky, means that I am part of the Cult of Listening."

The name clicked in Kluvier's mind. "The ones who climb up into the Singing Hills and listen for the voices of the gods?"

"We listen," she said, then added, "and we hear."

"But I thought," Kluvier struggled with the best way to ask the question. "I thought . . . there weren't any of you left."

"Not many," she said. "Just barely enough to keep up our vigil in the hills."

Kluvier was afraid to ask the next question but couldn't help himself. "You've, um, actually heard the voices of the gods?"

"Every day, one of us marches up the hill to relieve the other," she began, as if repeating a mantra. "We go to the top of Kapusshaw Peak. We sit. We are still. We listen. And we hear the voices of the gods."

What had Kluvier gotten himself into? Even Braax looked worried. "They've told you things?"

She knelt down in front of him, admiring the organ. "They don't speak in words, they speak in music."

Finally, something that he could dredge from his memory. "The eternal chord."

She stood and looked at him, surprised. "You know the eternal chord?"

"I mean, I don't *know* it," Kluvier said, "but I am a musician. The eternal chord is kind of a fairy tale in my circles. Nobody believes it . . ." he let his voice trail off. "You've actually heard it?"

She nodded. "The same chord, sweet and beautiful, has sounded through the Singing Hills for generations, while Neska thrived, peaceful and prosperous and strong. It was a sign of the favor of the gods. Yes, I've heard it. Many times."

Kluvier was about to ask another question, but she cut him off. "Come on, we need to get going."

He could have used more rest, but he also realized that it was better to get this over with. Once she had strapped back on the torch and he had the organ secured on his back, they started back up the path.

"What's so urgent that we get up there tonight?" He pointed toward the peak. "You said you've heard the voices of the gods, the eternal chord. If it's something you want to share with me, some kind of evangelizing, let's just call it a day. You can have your coin back." It hurt him to say it, but it was true.

She shook her head and kept walking, Braax nipping at her heels. "A few days ago, I went up the mountain to relieve my fellow acolyte. I sat and concentrated, focusing on the eternal chord. It was particularly windy that morning, so it was easy to do. I sat there for hours, reveling in the harmony, when, all of sudden, it changed."

Kluvier stopped. "It changed? The eternal chord . . . changed?"

She stopped and turned to face him. "Yes. Gone was the deep, rich harmony we'd come to know. In its place was sharpness, dissonance. Peace replaced by dread." She waved him on.

"That must have been amazing," Kluvier said, doing his best to close the gap to Shyana. "I mean, that's what your order has been listening for all these years, right? You must be thrilled."

"No!" She wheeled around on him, eyes glazed with incipient tears. "You don't understand! All these generations Neska has had peace and prosperity *because* of the eternal chord, *because* the gods willed it. But now, with the chord changed, it means the city could be facing disaster!"

Kluvier seriously considered leaving. He'd toss the bag of coin to Shyana and just walk away. Up to this point she'd struck him as a little out there, as you'd expect with cultists, but basically grounded. She'd clearly done whatever it took to get the coin and he didn't want to know the details. That suggested a worldliness that belied her status as an acolyte. But this was bordering on madness.

Still, something kept him from running. "There are other members of your order, right? Where are they?"

She started to say something, twice, then finally said, in a small voice, "they don't believe me. That's why none of them are here."

Braax barked.

"What he said," Kluvier added, hoping for some levity. "They don't believe you? Shouldn't it be obvious whether the eternal chord has changed?"

"They don't want to hear it. Haven't you ever known anyone who, no matter what they saw or were told, just didn't want to believe something?"

Kluvier knew the phenomena all too well. "But, isn't this what they've been listening for?"

"Not really?" she shrugged, then slumped down on a flat boulder beside the trail. "Maybe at one time, years ago, members of my order wanted to really listen to the gods. Now, of those that are left, I'm the only one who is willing to really listen. The others just do what they must to get along."

Kluvier set the organ down. Braax was jumping feverishly around his feet, so he picked the furry goblin up and started to scratch the back of his head. "Then what do you want from me? Do you want me to say that, yes, the chord has changed, that now it sounds tense and dreary? I don't really have the constitution for that kind of concentration."

"No," she shook her head, "I don't need you for the listening. I need you to help me do something about what we're hearing."

He rubbed the top of his nose, feeling a headache coming on. "How can I possibly do that? You're the one who dedicated her life to listening to the gods."

"But I don't know how to talk to them," she said, like she was admitting a deep secret.

"Talk?" Kluvier looked at Braax, who, for once, seemed more on the ball that Kluvier was.

"The gods talk to us in the language of music. I need someone who speaks that language to talk back."

Kluvier couldn't hold it in. What started as a snigger progressed to a chuckle and then to a full on guffaw. He laughed so hard he dropped Braax, who fell to the ground and popped up, chittering in protest.

"What's so funny?" Shyana asked. "This is not a laughing matter!"

Kluvier got himself under control, wiping a tear away from the corner of his eye. "It's not? It's completely preposterous! Your order, this collection of people dedicated to listening to the gods, aren't trained to actually talk back?"

She shrugged. "Maybe, at some point in the past, when there were more of us, some had the right training. The archives aren't well maintained and it was hard to find any record of anyone trying to talk back, but it might have occurred. I didn't have much time for research."

"So, what, exactly is your plan?"

She took a deep breath. "When we get to the top of the mountain, if the chord is still dissonant, you will play something."

"But you don't know what," Kluvier said, just to make it clear.

"I don't," she said, getting back to her feet.

He did the same. "What if I say something inappropriate?" He didn't really believe all this, but thought it was worth asking the question.

"I don't know," she said. "I just don't know. But I have to try. What if it's a warning? What if we can change what's coming?"

Kluvier didn't have good answers. He hoisted the organ onto his back and they once again started back up the path.

~

Kapusshaw Peak was underwhelming. Kluvier wasn't sure why he thought this, but he pictured the top of the mountain as jagged, rocky, and rugged, the kind of place where one false step would lead to death. Instead, it was much like the rest of the mountain, just flattened off. There weren't even any obvious rock formations of the kind that Kluvier figured were the real source of Shyana's gods. There was a consistent breeze, however, enough to ruffle Braax's fur.

It took him a moment to realize why the mountaintop seemed so artificial. It had been turned into an altar.

She must have sensed his disappointment. "It's not about what's here," she said, opening her arms wide. "It's about what's out there."

He supposed she was gesturing to the other peaks, the nooks and crannies, that surrounded them. At night, however, it just looked empty, with the high, wispy clouds blocking most of the light from the moons. Shayana put the torch contraption down against a rock in such a way that it continued to hold the flame aloft, like a skeleton.

Shyana smiled, just slightly, and held out her hand. "You need some convincing. Come."

He slung the organ off his back and gestured for Braax to stay next to it.

He took her hand and Shyana led him out onto the altar. In the dark Kluvier couldn't tell how close to the edge they were and should have been terrified, but Shyana's manner made him feel safe. When they reached the middle of the altar, Shyana sat and gestured for him to do the same. He got on the ground and crossed his legs under his rump the same way she did.

"Close your eyes," she said, like a mantra. "Close your eyes and let your ears open. Don't just hear, Kluvier—listen."

Kluvier closed his eyes. Listening was a natural part of what he did, but he thought back to a conversation with Andra about her conservatory days. He hadn't believed her initially when she told him that her first month there was spent just listening to others play. There had even been a few days when she was assigned to listen to particular rooms or performance spaces while they were empty. "You don't know how to fill a place with sound until you know what there is to fill," she'd told him.

He channeled that spirit, even if he knew he could never match Andra's concentration. He let his breathing slow and tried to empty his mind of thought and ideas.

It wasn't working. He could hear the wind, hear what he thought were dead leaves or other debris blowing across the rocky ground. He could even hear Braax back by the organ, doing that manic chattering thing he did when he was anxious.

Shyana must have sensed his frustration. "It will take a few moments, particularly for a lay person. Concentrate on nothing."

Kluvier did what he could, but couldn't shake the sense that there wasn't anything there to hear. How had he let himself get talked into coming to the top of a mountain, at night, with a woman who was apparently hearing things? The full coin purse on his belt felt even heavier with each passing moment. Maybe she would let him keep half if he walked away?

Just as he was about to give up, to stand and tell Shyana he was leaving, a sound started tickling his brain. It wasn't voices, or at least voices as he'd ever heard them, but if she had described them as singing Kluvier couldn't argue. He focused on it and several notes made themselves clear, most working in harmony, but a couple staking out odd intervals that gave the overall chord an undertone of menace and warning.

"I hear it," he said, softly, like he couldn't believe himself.

"Then you see," she said next to him. "That is not the sound of prosperity and peace."

"It is," he stopped, struggling for the words, then said, "unpleasant."

"It's ominous," she said. "Are you ready to try and change it?"

He opened his eyes. He still didn't really believe what he heard was the voice of gods, but something in the pit of his stomach made him question his lack of faith. "Is it really such a good idea to just try and talk without knowing what we're saying?" He swallowed hard, then added. "What if we make them mad?"

Without opening her eyes, Shyana said, "they're gods, not insolent children. Our only hope of possibly understanding them is to try and talk to them." Then she added, "trust me."

At this point, what choice did he have? "All right, where should I set up?"

She opened her eyes, but remained seated. She pointed toward an outgrowth of brush that appeared to be growing out of the rock of the mountain.

Kluvier went about his usual routine of setting up as best he could. Braax bounced around him as he did it, clearly as uncertain about all this as he was. But when the organ had finally been deployed, the furry beast hopped onto the turnwheel as usual and started to trot.

"It'll take a couple of minutes for the bellows to fill," Kluvier said, then added, "any requests?"

"Play," she said, then stopped, thinking. "Play something calm, something beautiful."

"Okay," he said, more to Braax then to her. "No reels or jigs, then, right?"

The beast barked his approval.

Kluvier started with a drone, a low bass note chosen at random that wobbled a bit as Braax sped up and slowed down in his trotting. Normally listeners wouldn't notice, but that's only because Kluvier didn't usually play long notes or chords. People wanted up beat and that's what he gave them. It was the nature of the instrument.

After a few moments of letting that one note hang in the air, he started adding others to create a rich, thick harmony. By the end, he was playing seven notes across the keyboard, the most he could manage without taking off his boots. He hoped that would do.

"No change yet," Shyana said, getting to her feet. "Trying shifting around a little."

He assumed she meant play different chords. Afraid to say the wrong thing, he dove deep into what little store of actual music theory he had and came up with the next couple chords in a progression that would keep the sound calm and majestic. It took considerable concentration to get all his fingers to do his bidding at the same time, but he made it. "Anything?"

"No," she said, some frustration creeping into her voice. "Keep going!"

He worked all the way through the progression once. Unwilling to try another, and risk getting it wrong, he returned to the beginning.

"Can you make it louder?"

Kluvier fiddled with a couple of knobs that controlled the flow of air from the bellows, then gave the turntable a swift kick. Braax went from a trot into a run.

"More!" she yelled, looking up to the dark sky. "More!"

"Give her all you got, buddy," Kluvier said to the little beast, who started sprinting like he'd never seen before. "I'm not sure how long he can keep this up!"

Shyana started pacing around the altar, head back, face to the stars. "Why isn't the chord changing! We're trying to make contact with you! Why won't you listen as we have these so many generations?!"

Kluvier focused on his hands, on getting the chords right, but still caught sight of something in the sky. Some kind of light, dim and distant at first, that appeared to be getting closer. As it did, the breeze kicked up to a full blown wind, threatening to blow Braax off the turnwheel. Dead leaves and dust started smacking Kluvier in the face.

The light grew and intensified until it was nearly on top of them.

"Why won't you listen to our plea?" Shyana roared as best she could over the music and the wind. She raised her arms to the sky in supplication. "Tell us what we must do! Tell us what is coming!"

The wind gained more strength and Kluvier couldn't hear his own music anymore. He kept the keys pressed and confirmed that Braax was wheeling away at full speed. If anybody could hear what he was doing, he couldn't tell.

"Talk to us!"

The wind shifted suddenly, blowing nearly straight down. It knocked Kluvier off his feet, sending him sprawling to the ground. Braax stumbled and fell off the turnwheel, but had enough of his senses about him to then run and dive into Kluvier's arms for protection.

The wind was so strong now that Kluvier couldn't hear what

Shyana was yelling anymore. He could only tell that she was shouting up into the sky, at the light. Then, as suddenly as the wind shifted again, there was a blinding flash and everything fell quiet. Even the wind stopped. All Kluvier could hear was Braax's wheezing as he tried to catch his breath. Overhead, the clouds cleared and the moons shone brightly.

"Shyana?" Kluvier said, getting back to his feet. He walked across the altar and back, but didn't see her. "Shyana?" He looked all over the top of the mountain for her, but she was gone. The woman who he had followed up here had vanished without a trace. He certainly wasn't going to stay up here any longer than he had to.

It was only then that Kluvier noticed the organ. The downdraft that had knocked him to the ground had splintered it into pieces. His livelihood gone, his way of life destroyed. He was on the verge of breaking down, overwhelmed by it all, when his hand fell to the bag of coin hanging from his belt. "Guess I know what I'll be spending this on."

He figured out how to wear the torch contraption strapped to his back, then let Braax jump back into his arms as they started down the mountain.

It was too warm in the recital hall of the Great Library for Kluvier to be wearing his long coat, but it was the only way he could smuggle Braax in with him. Since the events of last night the little beast hadn't left his side and had only now stopped shaking. The little guy liked music and Andra's recital would hopefully continue to calm him down.

Kluvier had gotten past the initial surprise and shock of what had happened, but was still wondering what to make of it. He doubted his senses, his memory. What he was in the process of convincing himself was that some sort of electrical storm arose and that, in the chaos, Shyana lost track of where she was and fell off the mountain. There were no gods, no dialogue, just a crazed woman and the idiot musician who needed the coin.

Andra was a sight, as well as a sound, to behold. She had the dexterity and grace that Kluvier could never summon in his own playing. It was almost like she had four brains all working one limb independently. Each hand danced across the three-manual keyboard, drifting occasionally to one of the stops or levers that altered the organ's tone. With her left foot, Andra operated the bass pedals, laying down foundational tones listeners could feel in their gut. With the left, she tapped out rhythms on a drum box, which featured several different chambers to provide different tones and pitches of percussion. Kluvier was secure enough to admit he was jealous.

The final piece on the program was a lengthy series of themes and variations, a few of which Kluvier could almost play himself. He'd heard it several times before and always anticipated the moment in the end where the variations resolved into the lush, ecstatic, main theme.

The final movement, the grand finale, involved a series of massive block chords, the kind that Kluvier thought might part your hair if you were sitting in the first couple of rows. Waves of sound washed over you as the piece came to a close. When Andra hit the first of them, Kluvier settled in for the finish, giving Braax a scratch on the back of his head. He closed his eyes, like he'd done on the mountain, trying to listen more deeply than last time he heard Andra play the piece.

The final variation began, a slow ratcheting up of tension as chords built one upon another, each one making subtle shifts in the harmonics.

He felt Braax start to shake again. He thought the little monster had calmed down, but he was definitely getting anxious again. Kluvier scratched him, without thinking, listening to the music, until he figured out why.

The chord Andra was playing was familiar. Not just familiar, it was the same one that he and Shyana had heard last night. It was the same angry, hectoring chord the gods had allegedly been using to communicate.

Why hadn't he recognized it last night? Not the particular chord, but the *type* of chord. It was the kind that a composer used to unsettle the audience before the sequence resolved into polite, regal harmony. It was the penultimate chord of the piece.

It was what came just before the end.

Kluvier did his best to get up without bothering anyone else, but that was hopeless once Braax hit the floor and started running, jabbering, for the exit. Kluvier followed as Andra finished the piece behind him, to well-deserved applause. He chased Braax out the door and out onto Claxton Green. In the distance, over the peaks of the Singing Hills, black clouds were forming. Not the clouds of a storm, of a cleansing rain, but of something much worse. In amongst the black swirls he could see flashes of light, sparks of flame.

He grabbed up Braax. Heedless, and knowing it was futile, Kluvier started running.

WHAT WE WERE TO ALICE

LIAM THISTLEWAITE

A dark cherry Mustang and a black Camaro collided, head-on, three miles past the entrance to Foxtail Drive in rural Virginia. It was hardly a two-lane road: in fact, it was hardly a road to begin with. Locals likened it to a stain, collectively smeared by tractors and ATVs across fifty acres of golden farmland.

Logan didn't know what to think. Was he the one to blame? The last thing he could remember was a nosebleed and the faint taste of iron at the back of his throat, a symptom of the dry heat. Next was a sharp turn around a cluster of brush followed swiftly by an airbag to the face.

By the time his ears stopped ringing and the muscles in his neck started twitching, Logan pushed down on the airbag and peered through his shattered windshield: he was going backwards. In reality, the black Camaro, nearly totaled, was creeping away from him in reverse. Its driver, a panicked silhouette, turned the wheel this way and that with trembling hands until the car stopped peacefully at the side of the road.

Logan killed his engine with a disheartening sputter and lifted his foot from the brake. His leg was sore— cramped and covered in goosebumps all at once. Moments later, his left arm reached for the door with a mind of its own, and he pulled himself up into the scorching summer heat with vertigo pulsing behind his eyes.

There was an endless wheatfield in front of him, and soft rolling hills around. His ears started to ring once more. From behind, he could hear a car door shut.

Logan turned, limping toward the Camaro with the sun in his eyes. Standing just past the ditch at the roadside was a teenager several years younger than Logan, hair and clothes disheveled, with a bouquet of red roses looking wilted and ruined against his Sunday best. Logan had a flower of his own in the passenger seat— a white tulip, plucked from the top of a casket earlier that day.

Logan thought the boy must have just been stood up on a first date, or perhaps he was running several months late to senior prom. Either way, his priority wasn't the crash, and it wasn't Logan: instead, he stared past Logan's car and into the horizon as if he never realized that the sky was so far away.

"Excuse me," said Logan, his voice cracking. The teenager covered his face with his hands and muttered something beneath his breath. A second later, he jerked his neck in Logan's direction— some kind of belated whiplash.

"Do you...?" asked Logan. His voice trailed off when he realized he hadn't thought of what to say.

He bit his lip and looked back at his car.

A total disaster.

"You have insurance, right?" Asked Logan. The kid looked up, shoulders shaking like an aftershock.

He muttered something that Logan couldn't quite hear. It sounded like a "yes", but it could have been anything— the kid's voice was soaked in depressive angst.

Logan rubbed his chin and sighed. The sun was getting lower, its color a deep orange. The teen laid his roses on the hood of his car and fished a cigarette out from the back pocket of his pants. He was nonchalant, despite his shoulders and despite the flushed look on his face. Logan watched him light the cigarette and turn his gaze to the Mustang.

"Do you have any signal out here?" Asked the teen, exhaling a puff of smoke.

Logan hesitated.

"I don't have crap," he said with another deep sigh, "except for a bigger freakin' premium."

The kid looked up at Logan, still smoking, with wide eyes.

"I'll show you my papers," he said, "and I can... I can write down my info, if you need it."

Something about the kid's voice felt earnest, almost innocent. Logan was annoyed, even more so with each glance at his car, but his anger was silenced by the poor smashed roses on the Camaro and a bloody stream trickling down from the teenager's nose, looking just as sad and painful as his eyes.

"Are you good?" asked Logan, motioning to his face.

The kid looked down, confused. He held his sleeve to his nose for a moment, then wiped the blood on his hand.

"I guess so... I didn't notice until now," he said. "Bumped my face on the wheel."

Another moment of silence. Another puff of smoke.

"You?" Asked the kid.

"Just dizzy," said Logan.

The teen nodded and lowered his cigarette, like he'd just been forgiven. Then, lethargically, he crept into the driver's side of the Camaro and leaned over to the glovebox. He re-emerged with a business card and a handful of insurance papers.

"That's my dad's office," he said, passing the card to Logan. "Call there later and they'll get you to my dad. He owns the car. I'll give you my cell, too..."

Logan turned the card in his hand, gold lettering sparkling in the sun. The kid held out his phone a second later for Logan to jot down his number.

(754) 944-9110. Nearly the same as Logan's, except for the area code. Logan thought it would be easy to remember, with hardly any need to write it down.

"And who should I ask for?" Asked Logan, taking the rest of the papers.

"I'm Dennis. Sorry."

Logan held out a hand. "Logan. Sorry we had to meet like this."

Dennis' hand was clammy and small. Logan didn't enjoy the handshake— he imagined it felt something like greeting a zombie.

Dennis turned around to release another puff of smoke; by then, a few drops of blood had soaked into the end of his cigarette. Logan examined the insurance papers, crumpled and faded around the edges. They weren't very helpful, but he was sure to acquaint himself with the insurance agency before handing them back. He couldn't help but notice the address alongside Dennis' name: some place in Fort Lauderdale.

"You driving here from down south?" Asked Logan, holding out the papers. Dennis tucked them into his pocket behind a zippo.

"Yeah," said Dennis, looking off into the wheatfield. Somehow, his voice sounded like his hand had felt— cold, and small.

"For a funeral," he said.

Logan never considered himself a busybody, but he was almost always privy to the town's "comings and goings". Rarely did his mother neglect the obituaries on Sunday morning, and rarely did she forget to mention them to Logan over Sunday dinner. There was only one funeral Logan was aware of: the funeral of Alice Donnelly, downtown, at least fifteen miles away. The funeral that ended twenty-five minutes ago.

Logan didn't want to be rude, but his curiosity was overwhelming. What was the likelihood of a funeral he'd forgotten about? It wouldn't have *totally* surprised him. He was forgetful, after all. Then again, how could he be sure that Dennis wasn't just passing through for a funeral someplace else?

After a moment's consideration, Logan decided that no common Floridian would casually find himself on a Virginian backroad like Foxtail Drive. Foxtail was nothing short of a secret passage, a road for locals with places to be and not enough time for the highway. All in all, it was the quickest route from the shopping center to the downtown business district, and there were no exits that led to anything but fields of corn, wheat, and mud.

Dennis was still staring off into the wheatfield, but now he was holding up his cell, desperate for a signal.

"If you don't mind— the deceased," asked Logan, a lump in his throat. "Were they local?"

Dennis shut off his phone and turned to face him.

"Yeah," he said, wiping blood from his lip. "A girl named Alice. Alice Donnelly."

Damn.

Logan felt guilty, with no idea how to break the news that Dennis' twelve-hour drive was apparently all for nothing. At the same time, he wondered how Dennis might have known Alice— in all the years they were together, Alice never spoke a word about some grungy kid from Florida with a rat's nest for a haircut.

"Smoke?" Asked Dennis, holding out a cigarette. He seemed calmer than before.

Logan thought about it for a moment, longer than he had allowed himself since quitting cold turkey.

"Sure."

Logan took the cigarette and leaned into Dennis' lighter. Slowly, he wandered to the roadside and rested against the hood of the Mustang. He knew that he should tell Dennis— he just didn't feel like it. Something inside him started to ache for Alice, a feeling he hadn't felt for a long time.

"I knew her. Dated her for two years, actually," said Logan, turning his head back at Dennis and the Camaro.

Dennis dropped his cigarette. Logan looked away at the wheatfield.

Dennis was silent. Logan didn't notice the look of surprise and confusion creeping across his face.

"Are you serious?" asked Dennis, his tone bolder than before. Logan jerked around to look at him, nearly frightened by the question.

"Uh... yeah," he said softly, "we ended things, like, six months ago I think."

Dennis' eyes, somehow, were even wider than before.

"I'm... I was her boyfriend," said Dennis.

Logan almost let his cigarette burn his arm before he could take his eyes away from Dennis. Who was this kid? When the hell did he date Alice?

The evening was getting cooler, but in that moment, Logan started to sweat. He didn't know if he should feel angry, sad, or something else entirely; and he certainly didn't know what to expect from Dennis. After a painfully long silence, Logan spoke up.

"So when did you meet Al—"

"Four months ago," said Dennis, interrupting. His eyes were pointed at the ground.

Again, Logan felt a sense of innocence. He wasn't sure if he should trust it, but he desperately wanted to debunk the possibility of an affair, even if it no longer had any weight. Judging by his answer, he got the feeling that Dennis wanted the same thing.

Dennis shuffled over to the Mustang with his hands in his pockets and a little less tension on his face. Logan took a drag of his cigarette.

"I met her online," said Dennis, finally leaning back against the Mustang. There was a small nostalgic grin beneath his bloody upper lip.

"I always thought it was a bunch of crap, online dating and long-distance stuff, but eventually I called her every night and..."

Dennis looked down, biting his tongue, his grin even wider. Logan's mind was elsewhere—back at the funeral parlor, back with that aching feeling.

"I met her on Twitter, of all places," said Dennis.

Logan looked over at Dennis and felt a tinge of anger. For a moment, he was harshly reminded of the fact that he was making small-talk with a grimy highschooler—some kid who demolished his car, in the middle of nowhere, who was likely one of the last people to ever speak to Alice. For a moment after, he was reminded that Dennis wasn't much younger than he was, and that they seemed to have more in common than he cared to admit.

The timing caused more strife than anything: Dennis and Alice, together, four months ago? Logan thought back to the argument at the steak house, the argument that most boyfriends and husbands dread above all. It was the perfect storm: a long day at college and a head cold joined forces to push the anniversary out of his brain. He remembered the reservation, painfully, but not once did he think of the occasion.

Alice told him something about distance, something about feeling alone and tired and not wanting any kind of company. Logan tried to downplay it, regrettably. Alice called him a complete jerk, and she told him that he wasn't everything, that she could take care of herself if he didn't care anymore. Logan asked why she cared so much, why an anniversary would even matter to someone "like her". He didn't know what he meant by that. He wanted to take it back, but he looked her in the eyes on the way home and decided he just didn't feel like it.

While Logan was lost in thought staring into the field, Dennis sniffled and wiped his nose. When Logan turned, he saw tears in his eyes. Both of them were quiet while an evening breeze swept through.

"I'll try my cell again," said Dennis, holding it up to the sky. He wiped his eyes and his nose as he did.

"It's okay, there's no point," said Logan.

Dennis lowered his phone and buried his face in the screen. Logan wanted more from him.

"When was the last time you talked with her?" Asked Logan.

Dennis looked at Logan, his head still low, taken aback by the question.

"I, uh..."

Dennis trailed off, his voice like glass.

"Right before she did it, I think."

Dennis wiped another tear from his eye. Logan sighed, his chest feeling heavier and heavier in a way he never felt when he broke up with Alice. He knew that Dennis was emotional, but he didn't care.

"Do you know how?" asked Logan, feeling embarassed. No one had bothered to give him the details.

Dennis didn't move a muscle. Logan licked his lips; his mouth had gone dry. After a moment, he knew Dennis wasn't going to answer.

"She left a note, sort of..." said Dennis, "texted it to me." His breath was stuttering and his eyes were red.

"I wanted to leave her something too, some flowers at least..."

Dennis was crying harder then, his head in his hands. Logan turned to look back at the roses, lying woefully in an orange ray of sun. Far past the brush and at least a mile down the road was a navy blue truck, slowly towing a camper in his direction.

"Might have some hope, man," said Logan, "there's someone else out here."

Dennis looked up, wiping his eyes just enough to get a look at the truck. The two of them stood quietly for a while, watching the truck go around the bends of the road until it reached the messy stretch full of hay bales, sticks and gravel. The truck stopped, naturally, and out came a friendly old woman with an offer to tow the cars out of the road and take both men to the nearest payphone.

While Logan thanked the old lady and gave her a twenty for the trouble, Dennis sat down at the edge of the concrete. Logan joined him while the lady prepared to move the Camaro.

"Funeral will be done with soon, I guess," said Dennis. Logan didn't care to explain that the funeral had been done for nearly an hour.

"I'll head back tomorrow morning. Live nearby?" Asked Dennis.

"Yeah. I don't live far from where Alice lived."

Logan extinguished his cigarette in the dirt.

"I'm sorry for... the emotions and all that," said Dennis, "it's just this car, and the..."

Glass tumbled down from the hood of the Camaro as it was towed away from the road.

"The kind of thoughts I keep having... I just wonder if there's something I could've done, you know? Something I could've noticed..."

Logan didn't know what to say at first. He picked at some grass with his fingernail and scraped some pebbles along the asphalt.

"I guess just think about what you did notice," he said, "some of the little things you might have done for her."

Logan couldn't help but recall the little things Alice had done for him—homemade cards full of glitter on his birthday, peppermint tea before bed. It all came rushing back.

"She did a lot more for *me*," said Dennis, reading Logan's mind.

"Lots of little jokes, little sayings."

A small grin returned to Dennis' face. Logan felt his stomach sink; he couldn't help but wonder if he'd been betrayed, if Alice had taken what was left of their relationship and auctioned it off to Dennis, piece by piece. Then again, if that was true, it was one more reason to feel sorry for Dennis.

As soon as both cars were taken from the road, Logan and Dennis sat in the bed of the old lady's truck and rode along over bumps and potholes for several miles, to the nearest gas station. The building had Wi-Fi, but there was still no signal. Near the dumpster and the icebox, there was a payphone. Dennis volunteered with a handful of pocket change to call a proper towing company.

Logan's mind was a haze, a dream of Alice in a whole new light, second-guessing everything: every smile, every laugh, every kiss. He wondered if he loved her now more than ever.

Dennis prepared to leave when the tow truck arrived and the payment was sorted. Logan scribbled down his cell on a piece of paper from the gas station and handed it through the window:

. . .

(757) 944-9110.

"Just in case. Hopefully insurance won't screw us over," said Logan.

Dennis nodded, browsing his phone, finally able to access the internet.

"And, you know... I think I'm starting to have those same thoughts too, but..." said Logan with a blue smile, "I think we'll both be good, right?"

Logan held out his hand for one last handshake before parting ways. Dennis chuckled and looked past him with a mindful stare.

"The last thing she said to me, her note," said Dennis, softly. His voice was oddly hopeful.

"It came outta nowhere..." said Dennis.

Logan ached more than ever.

"It said 'You were everything to someone like me.'"

The tow truck's engine nearly drowned out the sound of Dennis' voice, but Logan could still hear, like a whisper on the wind.

"She said something to me about that, but maybe it means something to you, too," said Dennis.

Dennis flashed an understanding smile and waved goodbye, motioning to the truck driver and making his own arrangements as the truck left the parking lot. It would return for Logan when the Camaro was taken care of and Dennis was someplace else.

Logan thought back to the girl he used to know. The setting sun was very low by then; he wished he could turn back time, feel the heat of the daytime, return to the funeral parlor— or maybe to someplace back in time. Only then did he realize he'd never told Dennis just how late he really was. It didn't matter, though: that much was clear. Dennis made it closer to Alice after she died than he ever had while she was living.

Something inside made Logan feel the same way.

LINLEY MARCUM

YOUEY'S QUEST

"Yeah, but...what's in it for *me*?"

Everyone knew the guy—Eugene the Minstrel, who could play but couldn't sing, and who everyone called Youey – sat across from Oronin, the wizard from Baxvons Cavern on the other side of the mountain. Youey ran his finger around the rim of his whisky glass as he narrowed his eyes at the old wizard. He lifted the glass and took a drink of the amber liquid, never taking his eyes off Oronin's.

"Well...I....uhm–"

"So, nothing?"

"No, not nothing!" Oronin's voice raised an octave. "Of course there's *something* in it for you! You and everyone you know will go on living! Isn't that enough?"

Youey watched him even closer. The old man looked around the tavern's common room at the other patrons as though he were hoping for some help, perhaps some support. The rest of the men in the room kept their heads down, their low, murmuring conversations provided background for the little drama playing out in the shady corner table.

"Then nothing."

Oronin sighed deeply and closed his eyes as he tried to keep his composure. Youey was just so damn *obstinate*. But, Oronin had to admit, he didn't *really* have much of an argument. He could go back to his cave and gather up his scrolls and crystals, but for someone like Youey, it wouldn't do any good.

Old paper and rocks, Oronin!

The portents all said that Youey was the one, though. He fit the criteria from every scroll he cross-checked, Had done everything - so far - they said he would do, and now? Well, the scrolls said that now was *the time*, and if he didn't go to the tower now, things would go very, *very* badly for the rest of them.

Youey slid out of his chair and crossed the room. There was a small raised platform with a single stool where his lute sat propped against the wall. He grabbed it up and sat on the stool and began to strum "Greensleeves" and sing tunelessly along. Oronin stood from the table and approached the bar. He dropped a single gold coin on the wooden surface and waited for the barkeeper to notice.

"I trust that will cover our drinks and...a little information, perhaps?"

"Aye, what can I help with?"

"Youey. I have a job for him. He's been quite emphatic in his refusal. This job requires a fair bit of travel, and I think that's what's got him, shall we say, reluctant to accept the position. Do you think you might have a word with him?"

"I s'pose. Don't know what good it'll do, though. I can barely get 'im in to sing these days. Seems he's in his cups more'n he's not."

"A shame, a shame. Surely there's someone? This really is the most dire of situations."

"Well, 'es ol' mum lives right near, you could try there. He lives there, he does."

"Wait, I thought he–"

"Nope."

"But all those songs, about his adven–"

"Nuh-uh."

"But he dresses like–"

"I'm tellin' ya, he ain't never been more'n five leagues from here, if that. He lives with his mum. Go right out the door, take the first left, go 'til you hit a square. Go out Scrubber's Close. You'll find 'er there. 'E learned to sing from her, you can't miss her, she wouldn't stop singin' if'n you paid her."

"Thank you." He tapped the bar a few times then left the tavern.

Even after he was out in the street he could hear Youey attempting to sing "Greensleeves."

At least the lute sounds good, he thought as he walked.

Newkenny wasn't a large town. It was no more than four streets wide by six streets long, and there were a couple of squares in town, and one large square near the town's center. Oronin walked away from the central square to one of the outlying squares that lay nearer to the town walls. He smelled the square before he came across the entrance to Scrubber's Close. The sharp, pungent scent of urine drifted from the opening of the close, and the sound of running water drew him into the shadows of the narrow alleyway.

In the center of the small square a large public fountain bubbled, spilling water into a square-shaped trough. Half a dozen women stood at tubs full of water and clothing, in various stages of washing. Piles of clean, wet clothes and soiled, dry clothes lay piled around the square.

There, in the middle of all the industry, stood Youey's mum, singing terribly at the top of her lungs as she beat wet fabric against the side of a barrel.

"Madam?" Oronin approached her. "Madam, a word please?"

The woman stopped both her singing and her beating of the fabric and turned to look at the approaching wizard.

"I can't take on any more work, love, I'm full up, I'm sorry."

"No, no, that's not–"

"Oh, I see. Yer a wizard." Derision colored her voice as she looked him up and down. "You do yer own warshin'."

"Yes, ma'am I do," he answered. He shaded his eyes with his hand against the harsh midday sun and extended the other for her to shake. "My name is Oronin, I'm from the other side of the mountain."

"I know who you are," she said. She returned to her work, twisting the fabric to wring the noxious-smelling concoction from its weave. "What do you want with me, aye?"

"I'm here about your son, madam. I...I have a job for him, but he's most adamant that he's not interested. I hoped that perhaps you could have a word?"

"Psha. Youey won't do nothin' I ask o' him. He's got his own mind, that's for sure! What is it you want him for, I might not want him to do it meself."

"Well, you see, I've read my scrolls and cast my portents, and *now* is the time for him to go on a… well, a quest, to be certain. He must go to… have you ever heard of the Tower of the Onyx Wood?"

The woman spat on the cobbles of the square, dropped the fabric to brush the front of her dress with her hands, and then twirled in a circle. Without a word she picked the fabric back up and continued her work.

"'Tis a cursed place. My boy won't be going there, no sir."

"Yes, yes, it's dangerous, but madam, if he doesn't go things could be much, *much* worse for us all."

"Bah. Don't care. Find someone else. I won't be tellin' him to go."

"It *must* be him, though! The scrolls, the portents–"

"Don't matter a puddle of piss!"

Her words brought Oronin up short. He watched her work for a moment and then, without further conversation, turned to leave the square. Youey's mum called after him.

"Oy, wait a minnit! Maybe there is something for Youey in yer quest, now that I think about it…"

Oronin stopped in his tracks and spun on the balls of his feet to face her. He narrowed his eyes and crossed his arms across his chest.

"How so?"

"Well, he's a troubadour of sorts, right? Ain't got no *true* stories to tell."

"Margie, hush it!" One of the women washing near her whispered, but loudly.

"We all know it's true, Ava, *You* hush it!"

The woman gave a *pfft* noise and went back to her work.

"You go with him, make sure he gets some stories to tell, I figure I can help."

"No, no, madam, I won't be going," Oronin said with a chuckle. "I've got uhm…business…here to attend to that I can't leave. This quest is his alone."

Margie said nothing and appeared to consider Oronin's words. After a few moments she shook her head and went back to work.

"Nope, you go too or he's stayin' wit me. Elsewise, go ask that Frazier boy. He's awfully loud about how he's some kind of hero. If you're stayin', go talk to him."

"That's not… that's not how this works, you can't just—"

"I can just do whatever I want, I'm his *mum*!"

Oronin turned back around with a swirl of his robes and left the square with his head held high. Halfway down the shadowy close, his shoulders dropped, and he watched the cobbles disappear beneath his feet as he walked. He headed back to the central square, somewhere he could sit and be alone with himself in a crowd, and get lost in his own thoughts.

He sat on a bench and surveyed the central square. People came and went with baskets and carts, some in through the street that led to the city's gate, some from the streets deeper in the town. All around him deals were being negotiated and made, and people carried goods in parcels wrapped in their arms.

"Is he still here?" He heard from somewhere in the crowd. "A man, in robes, have you seen him? Has he left yet?"

Oronin looked around at the milling crowd of people. A young, mouse-haired boy was asking anyone who would listen if they'd seen someone in robes, sometimes asking for a man with a long, white beard. When he received a negative answer he moved on to the next person. Oronin stood and set his sights on the boy, shoving his way through the people moving around the square. He found him with his hand on the arm of another stranger, earnestly asking (yet again) for a man in robes. Oronin gripped his shoulder and spun him around.

The boy was young—no more than eleven or twelve years old – and had a look of innocence Oronin hadn't seen in many years. Earnestness made his eyes sparkle, but made him overeager in a way that Oronin would quickly find annoying.

"It's *you*!" The boy said. His face blanched white and his eyes widened.

"If you mean Oronin the wizard, then yes, I am he."

"I'm ready! I've heard you're looking for someone to go on a quest." The boy danced backward a few steps away from Oronin. "Here I am! Let's go!"

"Boy, listen to me. I *can't* take you. I... I have someone in mind. Someone better suited to the que—"

"There *is* no one better suited than me! Why are we wasting time? Where do I need to go? What am I going to retrieve? Who do I need to see?"

"You need to go home, you need to retrieve some lunch, and you need to see your mum."

The boy dropped his head and stood in front of Oronin, his hands hanging limp at his sides. Oronin sighed and threw his head back, silently imploring the gods to give him *some* sort of guidance – any guidance at all – to deal with the boy.

"Listen, boy, what... what is your name?"

"Fletcher. Fletcher Frazier."

"Ah, so *you're* the Frazier boy."

"Yessir."

"You think you want to be an adventurer, then. Well. I think you're a bit young to—"

"But sir, I'm *not* too young! Take me with you, you'll see! I can do all the things you'd need an adventurer to do, and more! I can get into smaller spaces, and I run real fast, and... and..."

Oronin tried hard not to, but he laughed at the boy, who dropped his head again.

"Listen, Frazier, why don't you come with me. I could always use an assistant... or at least someone to run errands and clean up."

"Yahoo!" The boy jumped and thrust a fist into the air. "So there's hope!"

"Well, I wouldn't say that, but—"

"I know, I know. I'm coming with you though!"

"What about your parents? Won't they miss you?"

"Nah, they're gone. The orphanage won't miss me, either. C'mon, let's go!" The boy took off into the crowd and Oronin followed, going as fast as he could. The boy weaved in and out of the crowd and settled back in front of the Flighty Fairy, and Oronin could hear Youey's tuneless crooning as they stood outside the door.

"I have an idea," Frazier said. He peered into the darkness beyond the tavern's threshold. "If you're so determined to get Youey to go on your adventure, you need to offer him something besides your thanks. What's in it for Youey to risk life and limb for you?"

"Well, I mean... he should be proud to be chosen for this great quest, don't you think? *You* would be content with that, wouldn't you?"

"Of course *I* would be, but Youey... well, he's a bit more material than me. You need to appeal to his pride, don't ya think? You need to sweeten the deal a bit."

"I suppose. What do you suggest?"

"Well, his entire reputation is wrapped up in tales of adventure, right? Give him something to sing about. And give him solid proof that his tale is true."

"Hmmm..." Oronin crossed his arms and rubbed his temple with one long finger.

"What are you thinking?" Frazier asked after a few silent moments.

"I think it's time I talk to Youey again. But first... come on, we've got some shopping to do."

Oronin grasped Frazier by the shoulder and the two of them slipped into the shadows between buildings. The wizard looked around furtively, trying to make sure that no one was watching. Without looking at Frazier, Oronin extended his hand to the boy.

"Take my hand and don't let go." He said. Frazier grasped the offered hand and held on tight. Oronin recited a spell even as he continued to glance at either end of the alley. The air around them crackled with energy, and blue and purple lights arced between the two of them. There was a pop, and the world around the two of them lurched uncomfortably. Once his feet were back beneath him, Oronin walked briskly with Frazier close on his heels.

"Where are we?" Frazier asked.

"My home," Oronin said. He waved a hand and broke the illusion and a whole forest of trees melted into nothing, to reveal a doorway in the solid rock face of the mountain. With another flick of his hand, the door swung open and the wizard marched into the shadowy interior. As Frazier walked through the door, candles all around the room were come to life.

"What are we doing here? I thought you said we were going shopping..."

"We *are* shopping, my boy. Look for something—anything—that you think looks expensive. Go on, now!"

The two of them rummaged through Oronin's belongings examining and then discarding shiny object after shiny object.

"What about this?" Frazier asked, holding out a round gold

amulet intricately worked with ivory and obsidian. Oronin took it from him and examined it.

"Yes! This will do nicely, now let's go." Oronin grasped Frazier's hand and half-dragged him out of the cave. They blinked again and were back in the city, walking out of the shadowed alleyway and into the sun-drenched square. "Now, Frazier, where can I find an armorer? Preferably one that sells second-hand swords..."

He didn't wait for the boy to answer. He kept tugging him along across the square toward the quarter of the city where blacksmiths did business.

"I know someone, yes!" Frazier called from behind him.

It wasn't long before Oronin heard the ring of hammer against anvil. He stopped, and Frazier stopped next to him.

"He's just down here a little way," Frazier said after a few moments. "But why do you need him?"

"You said I needed to sweeten the pot. Well, I'm looking for some sugar."

The smith's stall was meager, but Oronin saw a couple of blades he thought might suit his purposes. Two in particular stood out.

"Smithy," Oronin called the stall's proprietor over, "I'm in the market for a... gently used blade."

The smith held up his index finger to indicate he should wait just a moment. He used the same extended finger to mentally catalog the blades as he passed them by.

"Sword or dagger?" He called over his shoulder.

"Just show me what you have, sir."

The smith took a sword and a long dagger from their display, gave them a quick examination, and laid them both on the table between himself and his customers.

"With either of these, how much more would it cost to have this," Oronin laid the amulet on the table between the blades, "attached to it? And can you do it today?"

"Shouldn't be much. Yeah, I can attach it for you. Prob'ly today. More likely be ready in the mornin'."

Oronin winced and met Frazier's eyes. It was clear the boy had no idea what to do.

"So, what kind of price for the dagger?"

"For that piece, with the gold thing attached to it, I could do... three gold pieces."

Oronin considered the offer for a few moments.

"I can do that, yes, but that's with no guarantee that it can be affixed today, yes?"

"That's right."

"I'll double it if you can have it done while we wait."

"Let's see the coin first, wizard."

Oronin dug into the hidden pockets of his robes and pulled out a felt pouch. He dropped six gold coins into his hand and held it out to the smith who picked them up, one by one, and tested them each by his teeth. Satisfied, he pocketed the coins, grabbed the blade and amulet from the table, and disappeared into the depths of his shop. He heard yelling and the ringing (from this smithy, at least) stopped. After a few moments it resumed with what Oronin perceived as a renewed fervor.

The wizard and the boy waited in silence, listening to the cacophony of industry all around them. Luckily, the smith returned before the silence became too awkward. Oronin examined the placement of the amulet on the blade. It had been carefully seated on the pommel of the dagger, and the work was so fine it almost looked as though it had been forged that way. Oronin was impressed. He handed the blade to Frazier, who whispered *wow* as he examined the blade.

"It will have to do, I suppose," Oronin said to the smith. "Split this among your men for their hard work." Oronin flipped a gold coin into the air and landed, flat-side down, on the table.

Oronin gripped Frazier's shoulder again and leaned down to whisper in his ear.

"Let's go boy. We'll have to hurry if we want to speak with Youey before the evening crowd gathers in."

Frazier nodded to the wizard then hugged the dagger to his chest. Without waiting on Oronin, he took off toward the Flighty Fairy. A glance at the sky told Oronin that he had precious few moments to get to the tavern, and as he drew closer he could already hear waves of raucous laughter spilling into the square from inside the tavern. When he reached the door he stood next to Frazier and without a word, extended an arm in silent request for the dagger. Frazier passed it to him.

"What are you going to do now?"

Oronin sighed deeply as he tucked the dagger into a deep pocket within his robes.

"I suppose I'll just go in and ask again," he answered.

"Well, go on! What are you waiting for?"

Another round of laughter erupted from within the tavern.

"Now. Come along, Frazier."

Oronin squared his shoulders, puffed out his chest, held his head high, and drew his hood over his head. He made his entrance between rounds of laughter. He hoped it had the right effect; the setting sun warmed his back, and he hoped his robes were fluttering artfully in the breeze. As he walked through the door he raised his hands above his head, palms toward the room full of men who sat around tables with their arms wrapped protectively around mugs of warm ale. At some point during the day a large, shaggy dog had wandered in and lay stretched on its side in front of the fireplace.

When Oronin stepped into the room all conversation stopped and everyone—the dog included—looked at him. When, after a few seconds he said nothing, the occupants of the room went back to their conversations, and the dog went back to his snoring. Oronin surveyed the room, frustrated. Youey sat at his corner table huddled in the shadows. His lute was across the room where it leaned against the tavern wall. He hadn't looked up when he entered the room, his attention fully on the ale he was nursing.

Oronin coughed and the room stopped again.

"Gentlemen, I am Oronin the wizard, and I am here to speak with Eugene the Minstrel," he announced. Some of the men in the tavern snickered at the man, some blew out derisive sighs, but one man silently pointed to Youey. Of course Oronin knew who he was, but he wanted to draw attention to his presence. He wanted people to know who *he* was and that he was talking to the minstrel.

Youey, however, didn't stir.

Oronin strode with purpose across the tavern toward the minstrel, and Frazier followed. When he reached the table Oronin pulled out the chair opposite the man and, adjusting the hidden dagger, sat down.

"Eugene," Oronin said. He waited for any response. "Eugene. Eugene. Youey."

The minstrel raised his head. He tried to look at Oronin but his eyes were unfocused and watery. When he realized it was the wizard who sat across from him, he rolled his eyes and allowed his head to fall onto his arm where it rested on the table.

"Youey, you don't have to look at me, just listen. I'm here to ask you again. You are fated to complete a quest. Will you go?"

"Shut up, old man," was his muffled reply.

"I looked at the scrolls and portents again, and you are the *one*, but I left something out. You are fated to take this on your journey." Oronin pulled the dagger from within his robes and allowed it to clank down on the table. Youey's head jerked up and he looked at the dagger even as his hands grasped either side of his head.

"Oh, gods," he said. He pressed his eyes closed and rubbed them hard enough that they made *squinch squinch* sounds with each stroke. "What in five hells is that?"

Oh no! I have no idea what it's supposed to be called!

"This... this is the last blade of... Randall the Barbarian," Oronin stammered. "I can't believe you've never heard of the... legendary... Ebon Sin-Pricker!"

"Of *course* I have! It's *only* sung about by minstrels far and wide! And Randall the Barbarian, how could *anyone* forget him?" He raised from his chair as he spoke, his volume steadily increasing until everyone in the tavern had turned their head to look at him. "I don't yet know the most recent songs, but I *have* heard them!"

Youey gripped the dagger by its hilt and held it out in front of him. Firelight glinted off the blade and caused Oronin's addition to sparkle brightly. Youey did his best to surreptitiously examine the amulet.

"Then, you should have *no problem* completing your quest to the Tower of the Onyx Wood?" Oronin was purposefully louder than necessary. A round of gasps circled the room, and an eager silence waited for Youey's response.

"Well, I... I mean I..."

"Yes?" Oronin prodded.

"It should be no problem at all, wizard. I presume you shall be accompanying me?"

"Oh, no, my boy, I won't be going. The portents and scrolls strictly forbid it."

A round of agreeing mumbling circled the room. Youey shifted his weight from foot to foot as concern wrinkled his forehead.

"Gather your belongings, Eugene the Minstrel, for you depart upon the morn!"

A cheer erupted from the tavern's occupants. Youey made his way across the room to collect his lute. A barrage of hands gripped and patted his shoulders, and there were calls for a performance. He finally made it through the crowd and stepped up onto the stage. The first notes of "Greensleeves" twanged from the instrument and Youey began to sing.

Satisfied, Oronin left the tavern (with Frazier hot on his heels) and popped back to his home. He helped Frazier move into his new home, then the two of them settled in for a good night's rest. Oronin woke before dawn the next morning and shook Frazier awake. The two of them set out for town, and popped into existence just outside the Fickle Fairy tavern. The two of them waited patiently for Youey to arrive.

"Do you think he'll show?" Frazier asked.

"I think his pride will permit nothing else."

Frazier giggled a little at this, but Oronin still had his doubts. He wouldn't put it past Youey to hide out for a couple weeks only to reappear with a new song or two about an adventure he'd never had. It truly shocked Oronin when Youey came stumbling around the corner, most likely still drunk from the night before. He led a saddled roan gelding weighted down with packs and a bedroll.

"I'm here, I've got the blade, now what?" Youey said. He slurred his words slightly, and his eyes were rheumy. The town was beginning to wake up around them, and a small crowd had gathered to see Youey off on his great adventure. "What, exactly, am I supposed to do at this bedeviled tower?"

"The scrolls and portents do not say, but they do tell me that you will know once you get there. Right now, you simply must undertake the journey."

"Pffft," Youey answered. He shook his head and rolled his eyes. He secured his dagger at his belt and mounted the horse. "Am I supposed to return here?"

"If you survive, yes," Oronin answered. Gasps came from the crowd, and Youey's mouth fell open in disbelief.

"What do you mean *if* I survive?"

"Well, there's always that chance, you know that. You take a risk just going to the tavern or helping your mum with the washing."

"Yeah, but...but..."

"No more of this, get on with it," Oronin insisted. Youey's shoulders dropped, but he turned the horse toward the town gates and urged him forward. A cheer raised from the crowd as he went, and Youey raised a reticent hand to wave goodbye.

"Bye!" Called Frazier. "Good luck, Youey, we'll see you when you return! You're my hero!" Oronin could tell Youey heard the word *hero*, because he sat a little taller and held his head a little higher as the horse sidled through the gates, headed toward the Tower of the Onyx Wood.

Frazier looked up at Oronin with his eager, annoying eyes. The wizard sighed and rubbed his temples.

"I suppose you want to know what this great quest was, yes?"

"Do you know? Can you tell me? What is it? What's he got to do?"

"Well, you see, a couple hundred years ago I lived with the enchantress of the tower. It was a...different... time for me, a bit... Well, we'll just leave it at 'it was a different time.' When I left, I forgot my favorite pair of socks."

"You can't be serious..."

"I loved those socks."

END

NESTING

MICHAEL FITZGERALD

I never used the small deck outside my apartment. Shortly after moving in, I put a table and two chairs out. With the traffic noise from the side street and occasional chatter from pedestrians, it was not an ideal place to relax. For that, I preferred my couch.

The deck, about 12 by 12 and fenced, was partially shaded by the large oak tree on the edge of the field of the rehabilitation facility across the street. There was empty space on it. I thought about adding plants but knew they'd wither when I would eventually forget to tend to them. There was no need for a storage building. Since I had no lawn, I had no lawn tools.

One night while relaxing on my couch, I reached for the remote and a pain shot up my back, a spasm, just like I'd had a few days before. It took my breath away. They seemed to be getting more frequent. I told my doctor about them and she said I should be stretching in the evenings, and to drink more fluids. I glanced over at my can of IPA on the table. At least I was following part of her recommendations.

I was certain the body aches were related to my job at the food and restaurant supply warehouse where I'd been working for the last year. We supplied businesses from hospitals, bodegas, to indie coffee shops. The facility was a huge refrigerator. You were always cold and your muscles never got to loosen up. I prepared orders for small mom &

pop shops. No forklift for me. I would run across the warehouse, dropping a few cartons on a hand-truck and wheel them to a staging area. Each item was then lifted from the hand-truck to a designated area, a taped square, for that order, as Dennis, the shift manager, stood, clipboard in hand, and ticked off each item. It was this repeated lifting and placing and lifting and twisting that turned my thirty-two-year-old body against me.

One evening, while in this state of discomfort, I saw the advert for a small inflatable hot tub. One hundred and forty massaging bubbles at my command, promising to relieve life's aches and pains. The unit would fit perfectly in the opening on the back deck, and the price was within my budget.

It only took a few quick clicks of the mouse, and by the end of the week I was inflating, filling and chlorinating my compact spa. Yes, this was more than a tub of hot water. It was a spa that would transport me to paradise, or at least to an environment where I had less back pain.

After checking the water chemical levels with the multicolored test strip, and still not having any idea if it was safe or a bacterial soup, I took off my robe and exposed my pasty chest to the world. I'd never stood on the deck in just my bathing suit. I felt naked. I played some music on my phone, entered the spa, slid into the 105 degree water, and laid back against the soft vinyl.

I noticed traffic noise from the main road a few houses away. It wasn't constant, but every once in a while a motorcycle or truck would zip by, briefly cutting the tranquility. But soon I drifted. An 80s prog rock song came on and I was relaxed. I pressed the bubbles button, and the motor came alive, overpowering the music. Those massaging bubbles engulfed me. My body swayed like a corpse in the river. This made me smile.

When I opened my eyes, I was awestruck by the sight of the sun going down behind this large oak towering above all the other trees. Its branches and trunk were like a skeleton, and the setting sun an x-ray. Briefly, near the top of this enormous tree, appeared a clump of branches and leaves. I took it to be a nest, though I saw no movement around it.

Just as quickly, the sun set and the leaves reappeared as the streetlights came on and illuminated the tree. As my eyes adjusted to the darkening horizon, I noticed small birds darting around. Little groups were swooping in and out of the evening sky.

My fingers were shriveling. I got out of the tub. The evening felt much colder when you were wet and nearly nude. I raced to put the lid on the hot tub as my suit got colder and stuck to my nether regions. Tomorrow night I would bring a towel.

By lunch, the day was already hell. Dennis was on a tear, screaming about every little thing. "Who crushed those eggs? Who smashed that bread?" If he didn't shut up, it was going to be, "who hit me with the hand truck?" He almost had Ivey, a three hundred and fifty pound thirty-year-old who breathed liked he'd just run up a hill, in tears and Coleton, whose life revolved around hunting, clutching his folding knife that he always had at the ready.

That evening, I pulled up in front of my apartment complex and parked in my assigned spot in front of the old oak I'd been watching the other night. In the day, you couldn't see through the leaves. Even from the bottom, the twisting branches blocked sight to the upper parts of the tree.

A scurry of squirrels darted along the sides of the tree, chasing each other as if playing a game of tag. They hopped onto the ground and scampered across the field toward the rehab facility, stopping occasionally to dig in the dirt. I glanced upward to where I'd seen the nest the other night. I couldn't see anything like it in this light. It was a good haul up that tree for those squirrels to get those nuts back up there if that's where they lived.

When I got inside, I didn't even wait for dark before stripping down, throwing on my still damp bathing suit and grabbing a towel from the cabinet. Shyness be damned. I needed to relax, and the world could just deal with my textbook "before" physique. I grabbed an IPA, pulled the cover off the tub, and stepped in. The spa heater ran all day, never giving it a chance to cool down. Ain't going to unwind in a kiddie pool. I needed sauna level temps. Soon I'd forget about broken eggs, forget about smushed bread, and maybe even Dennis.

The traffic on the main road was busy with people coming home from work and others just starting their evenings. I opted for some harder music to help mask the noise. After choosing 70s rock classics on my music app, I turned on the bubbles and laid back. It all blurred.

Next thing I knew, it was dusk, and I was waking up. The water was several degrees cooler since it used outside air for the bubbles and it had been on the entire time. I turned off the bubbler and the music. It was much quieter out here now. I took a sip from my warm beer and looked up at the oak now lit by the streetlight flickering to life. The only sound was the cicadas in the tree. Their constant droning surprised me how full and loud they were. How could I have missed that before? There must have been hundreds of them.

I watched the darkening sky for the chimney swifts. Surely they were out in force, ready to feed on these noisy insects. The sky was clear. I craned my head in all directions to catch their silhouettes against the evening sky, but saw nothing. Maybe it was too early for them? I didn't remember what time I saw them out the other evening.

I got out and pulled on my towel. After putting the cover on the tub, I went inside and changed. I had an hour to get everything ready before bed and another day of backbreaking work.

Fridays were the worst at the warehouse. The stores needed extra inventory for the weekend. Since we also stocked beer and wine, smaller businesses with not a lot of stock room ordered heavy on the weekend to keep up with the demand, knowing it would be gone by Monday. That meant I pulled larger and heavier orders non-stop on Fridays, often forgoing lunch, opting for something that could be eaten out of the hand while pushing a cart across the length of the warehouse. Not only did that give me an extra hour on the paycheck, all overtime at that point, but the portable meal would be selected from a pile of expired or damaged product that was free for our taking. Random and far from healthy, it would be enough to keep me going through the day.

At three o'clock, as I was heaving cases of Rebel Brew beer, a local low end yellowish carbonated abomination that cost as much as one can of a good IPA, my mind drifted and I daydreamed about the tub. The peach habanero jerky from lunch was digging a hole in my gut. I slumped over the handle of the cart. My stomach rumbled. My back ached. Quitting time couldn't come soon enough.

To make things worse, right at five o'clock, we got a rush order and had to stay to fill it. Usually I didn't mind the overtime, but not today. I was on my last thread and the tub was calling my name. I got home later than usual, and it was turning dark. Pulling into my usual spot, I glanced across the yard for the playful squirrels. They might bring a moment of joy on this dreary day. The area was empty. I got out and looked around the grounds. Nothing. I must have scared them off when I drove up. I went inside and nuked a dinner from the freezer. There was no time to cook a proper meal. I just wanted to grab a beer and soak. I'd let the sound of the bubbles and the drone of the cicadas lull me into a stupor.

The water felt great. I needed to check the chemical levels soon, I remembered, making a mental note. Ambient music was the choice for the evening, mostly for atmosphere. Something to mix in with the environment. I reached back to press the button to activate the bubbler and noticed the road noise was louder than usual. At this hour, it should have leveled off. I shut off the music and listened to the world outside the fence. Something was off. The cicadas were quiet. Not just quiet, but missing.

I knew the cicadas were out seasonally, but this seemed to be a short season. Maybe they swarmed and flew off for better housing like bees do?

I'd been sleeping better, more relaxed since I'd been spending my evenings soaking rather than veggin' on the couch, but something had woken me up last night, and not just a pee run. It sounded like a high pitch squeal from the tree across the street. When I poked my nose through the blinds, I noticed rustling in the branches near the top. It didn't last long.

Being a Saturday, I got to sleep in. I had a few errands to run in the morning and planned to get breakfast at the diner a few blocks away. I was in no hurry. As I walked across the parking lot, I noticed something unusual about my car. It appeared to be covered with a light coating of lint. I had completely forgotten about the activity in the tree in the middle of the night. As I opened my door, I saw a gray hunk of fur on the hood. I picked it up by a few strands. It was a squirrel's tail, tip to tiny bloody stump. I'd add drive thru car wash to my list of chores today. I never knew those rodents could get so terri- torial. That must be a prime location for a nest up in the tree's top. A location worth fighting for. I wondered if the tailless squirrel was the winner...or the loser?

I had my breakfast, did my shopping and got the car washed. Using a tube of pre-coated wipes, I sat in my car and cleaned the interior while I listened to music on the stereo. The music must have chased those squirrels away since the field was still devoid of all activity. When I finished, I walked under the tree and looked up into the center. It was so tall and the branches so twisted and intertwined, I couldn't see the top. There was no activity in the tree. No birds, no squirrels, no cicadas.

That night in the tub, I sat with the music low, staring at the tree. Another calm night with no insect sounds, no chimney swifts, nothing moving save for the leaves dancing in the slight breeze. What could have changed the environment of that tree so drastically?

I woke late on Monday and rushed to get dressed. You never knew how busy a Monday could be. Some places ran low on the weekend and needed a full restock, while others could make it to the middle of the week before calling. As Dennis would say, "Mondays set the tone of the week, so be here on time, ready to work."

I planned to pick up breakfast at a drive-through and prayed the line wasn't too long. When I got to my car, it appeared the hood was covered with paint. There was a large, whitish blob on it with a dark mass in the center. I let out an audible curse that could be heard down the street. I had paid twenty dollars on the deluxe package at the Thoroughbred drive-through car wash to have it ruined with...with whatever the hell this was.

I ran back into the apartment and filled a bucket with warm, soapy water. I didn't have any rags, so a retired concert t-shirt would have to do. Sorry Talking Heads, it's not like you fit anymore. As I poured the water over the mess and wiped it toward the front of the vehicle, the only thing I could think of was how much it looked like bird shit. But the size of this would have required a flock of birds to target my car at precisely the same spot.

Needless to say, I was late for work and Dennis was on my ass from the minute I hit the door.

"Eight o'clock means being at your station ready to work at eight," he bellowed, "not ambling up the street!"

I slunk my head as the others looked on, happy I took his wrath for the morning and not them. Each morning, Dennis chose one unfortunate employee to bear the weight of his disdain of life, and everyone's goal was not to the be the chosen one. For the rest of the day, I would have to stay out of his way and try my best not to screw up. Ivey grinned as he shuffled away from the morning meeting, knowing he was safe.

Dennis also scheduled our bathroom breaks, so we were never down more than one person at a time. That meant you got your bodily functions regulated or worked in agony. Trust me, lifting a palette of pinto beans when you needed to hit the bathroom will make you sweat.

During my nine-thirty bathroom break, I'd been thinking about what type of bird could have made the mess on my car, so rather than spend those precious minutes playing a video game on my phone while in the stall, I brought up a wildlife website.

Blue jays, cardinals, starlings, sparrows; most of the birds listed in this area were too small to make the mess I saw this morning. Down the page were the larger birds like eagles, turkey vultures and horned owls. I saw one that preyed on smaller birds and had a forty-six inch wingspan. I clicked on the picture and an animation of it played along with it screeching, filling the tiled bathroom with its call.

"That's a Goshawk," Coleton's voice echoed from outside the stall, as he turned on the water atthe sink. "I know a lot of guys who just watch porn when they take a dump. That's a new one." I think it may have been a joke, but I heard he got married in a camo tux. He always scheduled his vacation for deer season and his pickup, which you needed a step stool to enter, had both a gun and bow rack.

I exited the stall and washed my hands. "I have an enormous bird, well, I think it's a bird, living in the tree across from my apartment. I was trying to figure out what it was."

"It looked like a Goshawk?" he asked.

"I actually haven't seen it yet. All the squirrels have gone missing around the tree. There was quite a mess on my car this morning."

"A Goshawk might come in town for food, but they usually nest in a forest, not the city. They are aggressive and will go after squirrels."

"Let me ask you, is there any way for me to run it off? Chase it away?"

"Luckily it's not a," Coleton made air quotes, "protected species. If you'd like, I can run by and take a look. It'll cost you."

"What are we talking?"

"A six of Rebel Brew."

"Sure," I smiled. "It's cheaper than another car wash."

I slowed into my assigned parking spot across from the apartment complex. I considered parking in the visitor lot a half block away. I didn't want another bird crap episode like this morning. As I exited my car, I noticed none of the other vehicles had a drop on them. They didn't appear to have been cleaned recently, either. It was as though my car had been targeted.

That's when I heard it, the rumble of the exhaust pipes that were mounted vertically behind the camo painted cab of Coleton's Ford F150. He stopped next to me and smiled.

"Ready to get that sum'bitch?"

Like twenty dollar bungee jumping, I had a feeling this wasn't going to go well. I pointed down to the visitor lot, and he barked those thirty-five inch mudders, spraying the last pieces of pebbles embedded in the tread several feet behind him. Coleton hustled up the street with a hard shell gun case in his hand and immediately pointed to the oak.

"It's in there," he said. "It's up in the top of that, ain't it?"

"We're not going to do this out here, are we?" I asked, waving my hands around the nearby street and apartment complex.

"You want me to set up a hunting blind? Don't think anyone will notice that?"

"Come on!" I led him to my apartment. We went out onto the deck and were hidden from view by the fence. "You can see the top of the tree from here."

"Good thinking." He took out a small pair of binoculars and scanned the oak. "I see a hell of a nest up there. I don't see any activity."

"Something was up there this morning," I said.

"You saw it up there?"

"Not exactly. But whatever was up there left the remnants of its dinner on the hood of my car this morning."

Coleton stood on his toes to peek over the fence. He looked down at the parking lot, then up at the top of the tree and laughed. "You want me to send it a thank you note?"

He put the gun case down on the cover of the hot tub and opened it. Inside was a slender shotgun. "Nice tub," he admired. "My brother has one just like it."

"So, not a rifle or pellet gun?" I asked, risking ridicule from my lack of hunting knowledge. "This is a 410. I'm going to use a medium ball shot." He handed me a shell. "That nest is just a little out of range for its accuracy, but I will get a few balls up there. I'll fire two rounds. That's all we'll get before everyone hits the street. We'll tear down, go inside, and crack open those beers." This was me standing on the edge of the bridge as they tightened the harness, thinking of ways to get out of the entire situation. He wiggled his fingers for the shell I was clutching. I gave it back. He jammed it into the gun and racked the slide. Coleton looked at the nest through his binoculars one more time.

"Check the street," he said. "Let me know when it's clear."

I couldn't believe there's not a person out there. Not a car in sight. Just my luck. "We're good," I sighed.

Coleton dropped the binoculars on the cord around his neck and lifted the gun. Using the fence as a steady rest, he leaned back and fired. BLAM! It was shockingly loud. The sound reverberated in the enclosed patio area. Dust shook from everything on the deck. I might have peed myself a little. A second later, there was a peppering of the leaves at the top of the tree.

Coleton pumped the shotgun, aimed it and got off one more shot, just as loud. He ducked down behind the fence and pulled me down with him. The pellets tore through the leaves. Now doors opened and voices could be heard as people stepped out on their patios and into the street.

Coleton was casually cleaning the gun. I was more concerned about the police. "Do you have to do that now?" I asked.

"Always clean your tools," he winked. "Let's have that beer."

I heard my name shouted across the warehouse. I turned and Coleton was jogging toward me, dressed the same as yesterday, in camo. How did I never notice that before?

"That was wild, man," he said, holding up his hand for an expected high five.

"Certainly the craziest thing I've done since living there," I said, completing the five. I guess we're huntin' buddies now.

"Anything happen after I left? Any action from the tree?"

"A police cruiser drove past," I told him. "But there was no movement in the tree." The sad truth was that I did sit out on that deck all evening watching that tree. I didn't dare use the tub in case I needed to get out of there quickly. I finished that watered down Rebel Brew before turning in and woke every hour having to pee.

"Alright!" Coleton yelped. "I think we did it. Let me know if it gives you any more problems." Coleton slapped me on the shoulder. "Aww hell. Here comes Dennis. I better get to the dock." I rarely saw Coleton during the day. He worked stocking the racks when the trucks came in whereas I pulled orders. The warehouse was the size of two football fields; we were told. I really had no way of visualizing that. I marched on a football field in high school band. Maybe if I hummed my high school anthem as I worked, I'd have a better understanding of the scale.

As I was placing a flat of canned pineapple rings on the palette for the West Plaza bakery's order, a scream tore out across the warehouse. It must have been a one and a half football fields away from me, I guess. It was Coleton. I dropped the pineapple and ran.

In front of the stacks of instant coffee lay Coleton, face down. There was an occasional leg jerk, but he didn't look good. A forklift, with its lift cage still raised to the highest position, was parked in the center of the aisle. Its operator was frantically explaining himself to Dennis, who looked like he was about to stroke out.

Our safety director, whose medical training comprised of a two hour CPR combo AED course with a first aid kicker, ran out with a blanket and small medical kit. Coleton was screwed. When he rolled Coleton onto his back, he gasped. Coleton's eyes were missing. They appeared to have been clawed out. His face was a jagged mess. The safety director applied compresses to the larger wounds until the ambulance arrived.

Work stopped, and the police questioned the crew. Everyone had their own theory of what happened. I overheard the forklift operator telling the police Coleton saw something sticking out from the top of the rack. He lifted Coleton up so he could grab it. They figured it was a loose piece of cardboard or such. At the top of the lift, Coleton undid the latch of his safety harness and leaned out over the stack. That's when he heard Coleton scream, and he fell.

I walked back to my station to wait word from Dennis about the rest of the day. That section was taped off and OSHA was on their way. A shadow flashed on the floor from the ceiling skylight. I glanced upward and glimpsed a large object flying past the opaque dome. The shadow continued over the top of the building, passing each skylight. Then it was gone.

Work was called off early. As I left, they carted Coleton off in an ambulance to be examined. It appeared this was not considered a typical workplace related death. I looked to the skies before crossing the lot to my car. It was clear.

I drove home, jumpy at every shadow that crossed my windshield. I parked in my spot, put my hand on the handle, opened the door, and ran for my apartment. I sloshed through several puddles on the way to my apartment. Digging my keys out as I neared the door, I had them in the lock and it opened in record time. I was in and safely behind the door. I even let out a little "Whoop!"

For the next hour I paced, certain what happened to Coleton was payback for what he did yesterday. Did he injure what lived in the nest? Did it have offspring in there? This is the bungee cord snapping and me speeding toward the icy waters. My heart raced as I built more scenarios in my mind.

I opened the door to the deck and looked at the tree to see if anything was up there, waiting, watching. Instead, what I noticed was a missing hot tub. There was water everywhere and the pump, still plugged into the outlet, its hoses shredded and dangling from its side like an artificial heart torn from its patient, sat on the deck, whirring.

No! How was this possible? There were no signs of the tub anywhere on the deck. Then I heard a sound in the sky. Could it be wings flapping? Starting as a black dot, it got larger and headed toward me. It was mostly obstructed by the sun, but there was move- ment. I wanted to run inside, but also needed to see it, needed to face it. I turned to the door to judge how much time I'd need to make it safely to the apartment before it reached me.

As it closed in, I noticed its path was not at me, but at my car. It was dropping straight at my car. When it cleared the glare of the sun, I finally realized what it was, not some large winged creature, but my hot tub falling from the sky. It landed on the top of my car, crushing the roof and blowing out several windows. The car alarm went off.

I walked back through the apartment and outside, through the pools of water that were the lifeblood of my once luxurious spa, which now sat on top of my car like a cheap toupee. I pressed the button on the key fob to quiet the alarm.

I walked under the tree and spewed a string of obscenities that would make a sailor blush. I cursed the inhabitant of the nest. I cursed the tree for housing it. I cursed nature itself. That's when it replied. A screech that made the hairs on the back of my neck stand up. A screech to let me know it was in charge. It was the alpha here.

The top of the tree trembled. Was it about to attack? If I ran for my apartment, I would be in the open. That was where it had the advantage. I'd never make it to the door. I looked at the entrance of the facility behind me. It was surrounded by smaller trees. That would be a longer run, but it wouldn't have the open area for attack.

I chose the latter, running under the cover of the other trees. The branches at the top of the oak began violently shaking. Smaller limbs and leaves fell onto the cars parked below. I focused on the door sign listing the visitor hours. It seemed so far away. Almost a football field's length, if I were to guess.

Then I heard the first flap of its wings. It could have been a sail cloth of a mighty ship catching the wind. A loud pop as its wings fully opened. It was closer than I realized as it dug its talons into my upper back and latched onto me. With another powerful flap, my feet were no longer on the ground. I was still trying to run, but just caught air. The pain became unbearable. The doors to the rehab facility blurred.

A shotgun blast brought me out of my stupor. I veered to the side, and we both crashed to the ground. The next thing I recall was a man with a camo ball cap slapping the side of my face. His partner was dragging a massive object away toward a brute of a pickup truck.

"They're coming from the facility for you," he said. "You'll be fine."

He stood and walked away.

"Who are you?" I muttered.

"I'm Dale. We're Coleton's brothers," he said. "We'll take care of this."

As I began to fade out, I saw them heft the animal into the back of the pickup and the sky filling with thick black smoke as it pulled away, as though they were driving it straight to hell. Two nurses knelt over me, asking me questions I still don't recall answering.

I wasn't out of the hospital in time for Coleton's funeral, and never got to thank his brothers or ask them what it was they killed that day. I spent weeks explaining it all to my insurance company. It would be months before I could use a hot tub, so I bought a gas grill to put in its place. For my first meal home, I made chicken. It was delicious.

BOREALIS

MIKE HORNYAK

You went to Alaska to see the northern lights,
hoping to find some answers or absolution in that shimmering impos-
sibility.
But there was nothing like that there.
It was just another place you couldn't stay —
one more town you had to leave,
beckoned once again to the workaday.

Thin layers of gas, science and hope —
an insipid, tattered fabric —
separated you from the oblivion you secretly crave.
You could almost touch it.
You could almost float away,
wrapped in those undulating, luminous ribbons.
You could almost drown in its fluttering, seductive rivers.
Almost.

You say you'll travel where angels fear to tread.
A presumptuous claim, though you'll never understand
the cliché:
A grand adventure,
a glimpse at the face of danger,
like peeling back a facade and revealing its maker.

But pissing into the wind carries its own consequences.

Really, you're a little kid —
scared, and talking big to keep the monsters away.
But even the monsters know that a peacock's feathers
aren't dangerous.

They aren't new to posturing, they simply aren't interested.
Webs collect between the tired old planks of your fences.
Methodical segments catch the dew
and dance the sunlight along the delicate strands.
But all homes house a possibility of predation
and you wipe them away.
Those houses weren't as important as yours.

Ferns grow at the corner of your yard.
They remind you of a book you read when you were young.
Fronds have names like feathers on a wing,
but you've never cared for minutiae.

HIGH THE CASTLE WALLS

MIKE HORNYAK

raise high walls 'round the castle
hedge the walkways and strengthen the gates
expand the borders and fortify the boundaries
so no one can enter
       no one can see
so I may walk in my gardens
and know these hazy hills are mine alone

THE WIND, THE SEA, THE MOON

MIKE HORNYAK

This crimson thread reaches and tangles.
Doesn't it?
This string, tied each to my little finger and yours,
an oath and a law; a sacred predestination.
     This ascot, the color of a twilight sky,
       billows frantically as I fly,
           free and soaring, shedding all boundaries.
     Though I gladly yield to this tether,
         for you wait at its end.

There must be a moment when lovers can rest
and find a place they belong.
     And now
        for you
           I dream a winding web of home

The hubris of our convictions caught up to us.
Didn't they?
Those manacles, strong and binding, broke to pieces,
scattering our very purpose through the stars.
     Your hair, the color of a stormy sea,
       faded like wave-spray into the undeserving air -
          the last thing I could see while destiny folded in.

There must be a moment when warriors can rest
and find a place to be at peace.

      And now
            for you
                  I sing a winding web of home

I ripped my voice and tore my flesh.
Didn't you?
But these broken bones, a labyrinth of cracks and shatters,
will heal like my deep bruises and battered pride.
        The moon and the tide dance an unyielding dance -
            the wind warbles a melody of their romance.

There must be a way we can find ourselves again.

      This song
            for you
                weaves a winding web to home

THRIFT STORE

RUTH STANLEY

At this point, I'm a bit of a thrift store find.
I've been recycled, manipulated, and reused.
You can find me at the rummage sale without a price tag.
Strangers will talk me down to a more desirable amount.
My soul will be sold to the next individual.
Rinse and Repeat.
They will return me once they get bored.
Back on the shelf to be advertised again.
They view me as completely worthless.
But maybe I can be the replacement.
Does she drown herself in vodka and tonics like me?
Nose scrunched up as the powder surges into the blood stream.
But the drug- induced self-confidence made me harness my power.
My future lies with the highest bidder now.
Second-handed shop metamorphosed into Gucci.
Money is the only way to "own" me and I'm expensive.

GROWING UP ON GOVERNMENT CHEESE

SHELLY JARVIS

It's early,
But Mama's already ankle deep in baby tears
I skip past the crying thing to my Apple Jack's
munch a few before I make my escape
to the yard.

blonde haired monster in blue jeans
chasing Amy through the trees
seems like only a minute
til Mama calls me back
for grilled cheese and tomato soup.

That grouchy Oscar is up to no good on his Street
as I drink my bottle of cola
"These are the Days of Our Lives"
it says, and when I hear those words
I know it's time to go and play

Jeremy eats the dirt today
and I laugh so hard I cry
Dance down to the creek to look for turtles
til I see that sun set and wander
back home muddy and wet.

Baby is sleepin' already when I come inside,
Mama is sittin' at the table crying
over some papers, wondering if we'll have dinner tomorrow.
Daddy's gone workin' over the road,
and I don't know how to make her stop being afraid.

Mud pies still taste the same,
and crayons still color.
Play-dough gets stuck in the carpet no matter where you live.
Growin' up poor ain't nearly as bad as people think,
not when you got that government cheese.

MOTHER

SHELLY JARVIS

I am mountains,
cold and hard against the clouded sky,
where roots live long twisted lives within me

I am trees
holding on to things that once were soft and easy
now grown rough and strong through years of work.

I am valleys
built between majestic peaks,
a harbor for the weary, a home for the workers.

I am streams
trickling, running, racing down and down and down
through open, closed, and covered places.

Wind touches me,
whispering in my open ears.
She carves her name in the history of my lands.

I am grass
responding to the soul of the wind,
blowing, flowing, rustling night and day and night.

I am sky
pushing down upon the earth,
finding my place among the things that live.

TRILLIUM

TRACY SEFFERS

I cannot unsee them, the ragged cast-off underwear, soaked by rain,
fully indwelt by now, home to pillbugs, beetles, delicate fungi.

I cannot unsee it, the small canister of cheap cologne rusting beneath
a clot of plastic bags and fetid socks half-decayed into dirt. Lucky
You, it says.

I cannot unsee her, in that place where my mind wanders derelict and
willful, halo of dark tangled hair spread over a pillow of rotted leaves,
a disheveled crown

marking her queen of this musk-laden night. She stares up through
vine-choked sycamore to lock eyes--not with whatever lover ruts
drunkenly upon her body—

but with the moon, high and untouched by the damp humus now
soaking into her last clean shirt—just another piece to be cast off in
these woods—

easier to throw away than to find a place to wash. Thus too with used
wipes, tampons, condoms; and of course the underwear, crusted with
old blood and semen and shit—

THE PHOROPTER'S GLASS

TRACY SEFFERS

Notoriously weak-eyed, we know all about the Phoropter, don't we?
that half-magical half-steampunk optometrist's tool,
faceplate of a hundred lenses, a hundred and one foci,
spinning our squinty astigmatic eyes up to a crystal clarity.

That night, I brushed it away as I watched you sleep, holding your hand -
Thunk! – a lens fell, and your hand was only two years old, tiny and cool,
and – snick! – my hand was my mother's. I turned to see your face,
haggard and sad, chin and neck smeared with blood drying brown, and

– click! – now your newborn mug, indignant, smeared with a different blood -
my own this time, your first and most fiery baptism. What I wouldn't give
to trade lenses with you – to let you see through my eyes. What I wouldn't pay
some optometrist to say, instead of "Is this one clearer? Or this one?" to ask instead,

of each lovely filter of memory: "Is this more beautiful? Is this truer?
Do you see love more clearly here? Is hope easier to make out with this one?"
Where does that magic live, except in the tired eyes of a mother sitting in the ER
next to her son, in the tears of a father sitting in silence at home, trying to ignore the vision

waiting in his ravaged heart for the next unguarded moment. There's magic in this town,
son, and we are calling it down all around you, do you see it? Is it clearer now?

www.ingramcontent.com/pod-product-compliance
Lightning Source LLC
Chambersburg PA
CBHW030941310726
48969CB00008B/2338